Cooking Spirits

An Angie Amalfi Mystery

JOANNE PENCE

QUAIL HILL PUBLISHING

Quail Hill Publishing
PO Box 64
Eagle, ID 83616

Visit our website at www.quailhillpublishing.net

First Quail Hill Publishing Paperback Printing: April 2013

10 9 8 7 6 5 4 3 2

ISBN: 0615779417
ISBN-13: 978-0615779416

Here's a Taste of Some of the Praise for
Joanne Pence's Angie Amalfi Mysteries

"Angie Amalfi is the queen of the culinary sleuths."
—*Romantic Times*

"A winner...Angie is a character unlike any other in the genre."
—*Santa Rosa Press Democrat*

"A tasty treat for all mystery and suspense lovers who like food for thought, murder and a stab at romance."
—*The Armchair Detective*

"Joanne Pence is a master chef."
—*Mystery Scene*

"Pence can satisfy the taste buds of the most skeptical mystery reader."
—*Literary Times*

"Singularly unusual characters...fervently funny."
—*The Mystery Reader*

"A wicked flair for light humor...a delightful reading concoction."
—*Gothic Journal*

"Another terrific book...a bit of Lucille Ball and the Streets of San Francisco"
—*Tales From a Red Herring*

"Murder couldn't be served up in a more delicious manner."
—*The Paperback Forum*

"...the humor, the wit and the satisfying twists of this romantic tale... just the right measures of intrigue, danger, jealousy and warmth."
—*The Time Machine*

To Michaela and Matthew

A Note from the Author

Dear Reader,

Six years have passed since the last Angie Amalfi mystery (which was the fourteenth book in the long-running series), and I would like to thank the many people who have written to me to ask for another story. Because it's been so long between books—and because I hope many new readers will give this story a try—I've done my best to introduce each character so that no one will feel lost as to who's who, or what has gone on in the past.

In a nutshell, Angelina Rosaria Maria Amalfi, the youngest daughter of a large, wealthy San Francisco Italian-American family, wants only two things in life: a good job in the culinary field, and San Francisco Homicide Inspector Paavo Smith. Her relationship with Paavo is progressing, albeit slowly, since they met in the first book in the series, Something's Cooking, *which was written as a stand-alone 'romantic suspense' and not as a mystery (I point this out because true mystery readers will find it easy to solve!). Since readers were interested in what happened next to the couple, the mystery series was born.*

In book 4, Cooking Most Deadly, *Angie meets Connie Rogers who becomes her best friend, as well as three ex-cons who (some say) bear a close resemblance to The Three Stooges.*

Paavo is a bit of a mystery man (what kind of a name is Paavo Smith, anyway??) and Angie doesn't learn his background until book 8, To Catch a Cook.

Connie tells her story in If Cooks Could Kill, *the 10ᵗʰ book, and Angie's neighbor, Stan Bonnette, stars in book 12,* Courting Disaster. *Angie goes international in book 14,* The DaVinci Cook.

And throughout all are Angie's struggles with love, life, crime and cooking.

For some people, characters in novels are just that— words on a page. For me, after (now) fifteen books with Angie and Paavo, I prefer to think that somewhere 'out there' is an alternate universe where Angie, Paavo, their friends, family, and co-workers live and are every bit as real as you and I. If that were the case, and if Angie came to my door, I'd gladly invite her in for a cup of coffee and Italian cookies, and we'd talk about her latest adventures and, of course, Paavo...

I hope you enjoy this story, as Angie goes house-hunting with some 'spirited' results.

Sincerely,
Joanne Pence

Cooking Spirits

Chapter 1

Angelina Amalfi had no sooner entered her penthouse apartment high atop San Francisco's Russian Hill than she heard a knock on her door.

"I was just thinking about you, Angie," her neighbor, Stanfield Bonnette, said as he entered the apartment. "And then I heard you come home. You look tired."

"I am tired." She tossed her Balenciaga jacket on the arm of a chair, kicked off her Jimmy Choo four-inch high heels, and plopped herself down on the sofa.

Stan sat beside her. He was thirty, thin and wiry with light brown hair and brown eyes.

His was the only other apartment on the top floor of the twelve-story building on the corner of Green and Vallejo Streets. Stan could afford his place thanks to his father, a bank executive. He had a job in the bank for the same reason. Neither provided much motivation for Stan to work hard, or to work at all for that matter.

His one regret in life was that Angie wanted to marry someone who wasn't him. He thought they'd be perfect together—her money and what he saw as his self-evident charm. He continued to hold out hope that someday Angie would come to her senses and dump her fiancé, San Francisco Homicide Inspector Paavo Smith. Stan was ready, any time, to take his place.

"I just fired the worst wedding planner the world has ever known," Angie said.

"You fired her?" Stan couldn't imagine getting up the nerve to fire anybody. "But I thought you needed someone to help you with your wedding."

"I do! That's the problem!" She leaned forward and rubbed her temples. "But she kept pushing a wedding dress cut too low with a bouffant skirt that puffed out at the waist. I'm short. I've been clothing this short body for many years, and so I know that with so little material on top, and so much on the bottom—the skirt was wider than it was long—I would look like a marshmallow, a miniature marshmallow, and I did! The dress swallowed me up completely, but she insisted it was perfect and I 'needed' to buy it without letting my mother or sister or anyone else give an opinion. She said families only confuse the bride."

"That may be true," Stan murmured, giving a shudder at the mention of Angie's mother and sisters.

"And then, she thought the reception should be decorated in blue. I'm not a blue person. I'm Italian!"

She heaved a sigh. "Finally, I realized the only thing I 'needed' was a new wedding planner. One not so bossy!" She picked up one of the See's chocolates in the candy dish on the coffee table and took a bite, chewing morosely. Raspberry cream. She didn't even like raspberry cream, but ate it anyway. She was truly miserable. Wedding planning was a stress test and she was losing.

Stan also ate one, and wandered off to the kitchen as he licked the chocolate off his fingers.

"This isn't going the way I want, Stan," Angie called.

"What am I going to do?"

"Tell you what." Stan's voice sounded muffled, his head inside the refrigerator as he perused the left-overs. He always said he could get better food eating Angie's leftovers than at some of the most expensive restaurants in town. "Why don't I help you cook dinner tonight? After we eat, you'll feel a lot better, I'm sure."

Despite his words, Stan couldn't cook. "Go ahead and eat whatever you'd like, Stan. Paavo's coming over later, and we're going out to dinner." She took another chocolate, this one a caramel chew, as she thought about her handsome fiancé. She loved everything about his looks from his thick, dark brown hair, to his high forehead, penetrating light blue eyes, high cheekbones, and aquiline nose with a small jog in the middle where it had been broken more than once. He was broad-shouldered, his body long and lean, and everything about him exuded power and, to her, more sexiness than any one man should possess.

The whirring of her microwave pulled her from her daydreams.

She reached for a third chocolate, a pecan butter cream, her favorite. Before this wedding was over, she will have learned what was inside each chocolate just by looking at the swirls on top. "This is all making me so nervous, I'm putting on weight. I haven't even settled on my bridesmaids yet. Do you know how many sisters and cousins I have? And they all expect to be part of the wedding. At the same time, Paavo keeps saying he wants a small wedding. You know how much he hates crowds. It's a nightmare."

"It'll all work out." Stan put a placemat on the dining room table and in another minute carried a plate with two pieces of Chicken Kiev.

"You can make yourself a salad or some broccoli as a side," Angie suggested.

"No, no. This is fine. I wouldn't want to overdo it." He cut into a piece and hot, garlicky butter oozed onto his plate. One bite and he was in heaven. "I tell you, Angie, if you were marrying me, I'd be home every night for dinner."

"I know." One of the ironies of her relationship with Paavo was that his busy schedule often caused him to work late into the night and miss dinner. At the moment, he had no complicated cases that she knew of, which meant he should have time to help with their wedding plans. "I hope, once we're married and living together, we'll share more meals. That reminds me, I've got to clear out some of my things so he'll have room here."

"Oh my God!" Stan put down his fork before he'd finished, a remarkable thing for him. "You aren't saying he's moving into this apartment, are you?"

"Of course he is. I can't fit into his house. It has only one bedroom, one bathroom. Not even a dining room."

"Angie, you can't expect him to live in your father's apartment building!" Stan said, digging in again with gusto to make up for lost time.

Angie had already recognized that it wasn't a stellar idea, but she hated hearing Stan say it. "My father might own the building, but we've always considered this to be my apartment. I'll clean out the den and make it Paavo's 'man cave.' He'll like that."

Stan took another bite, savoring the rich flavors as he digested the information. "But if you do that, where will you put your desk and computer and all the books you have that you've used to start businesses?"

"For all the good that's done me!" Angie interrupted.

Now, she was not only tired, but dejected as well. Her inability to create a rewarding career for herself was one of the banes of her life. She had a talent for cooking, but even though she had tried to become a cake baker, candy maker, newspaper food columnist, restaurant reviewer, took part in a radio cooking show *and* a TV cooking show, and on and on...nothing ever worked out.

Stan frowned as he savored the last bite of Chicken Kiev. "It's not going to work, Angie. As a man, I can tell you that Paavo will not be happy here. If I were him, I'd hate living in your apartment. In fact, I'd do everything I could to postpone the wedding just to avoid it. Just wait. He's going to try to back out of this. First step will be breaking dates with you, and then he'll start suggesting the wedding be postponed. You'll see."

"Paavo never breaks dates with me...unless he has no choice because of a homicide, which is perfectly understandable," she said, glaring fiercely. "Fortunately, you're nothing like Paavo."

He sniffed. "No. I tell you exactly what I'm thinking; Paavo doesn't. He doesn't want to upset you so he'll suffer in silence, growing more and more unhappy every day until, finally, he'll walk out on you!"

"Nonsense!" she said, but even as she said it, she knew Paavo held things inside if troubled. He would turn quiet and distant instead of blathering and complaining the way she did. When she first met him, she thought he was cold because of that. Quickly, she learned how much he felt—sometimes too much.

Stan put his plate, fork and knife in the dishwasher. "He'll deny it, but that doesn't mean he'll like being here."

Angie fumed. How could he think he knew more about Paavo than she did? And yet, Paavo never actually said he wanted to move into her apartment, just that he agreed she couldn't fit all her stuff into his little house. "I'm busy, Stan. Why don't you go home?"

He poured himself a generous glass of the Beringer Petite Sirah sitting on the counter. "You can kick me out, but that doesn't mean you should ignore my advice." Holding the glass high in the air, he headed out the door. "I'll bring it back next time."

She folded her arms and sat back on the sofa, not sure if she was more irritated at Stan or herself, as she glanced at the half-empty box of chocolates. But she couldn't stop the question reverberating in her head: *What if Stan was right?*

Homicide Inspector Paavo Smith walked into Katie Kowalski's house holding the hand of Katie's young son, Micky. Katie was the widow of Paavo's first and long-time partner in Homicide, Matt Kowalski. They had gone through the police academy together and had been best friends.

After Matt had been killed in the line of duty, Paavo made sure he visited Katie and spent time with Micky at least one Saturday or Sunday afternoon each month, and often two or three times a month. He particularly enjoyed taking Micky to a park, to baseball games, playing sports with him, and doing at least some of the things he thought Matt might have done with his son if he had lived.

Katie stood in the living room of the small house to greet them. "Welcome home!" she said. "Micky, why don't you go wash up and change your clothes! You look like you fell into a pig sty!"

"Aw, okay. Bye, Uncle Paavo! Thanks for everything!"

"Bye, Mick! See you soon."

Paavo faced Katie. "The field had a few mud-puddles from last night's rain, and Micky found every one of them. Often on purpose. But I think he'll be feeling pretty good about himself when he joins that T-ball team next week. If you'd like me to take him, I'll do my best to get off work on time so I can."

Katie didn't answer right away, but looked at the floor a moment before lifting her gray eyes to his blue ones. "Paavo, I don't know how to say this. I appreciate all you've done for me and Micky, but I'd like you to stay away...for a while, at least. I've met someone."

His brow furrowed. He had expected this day would come, but not so soon. "Who?"

"It doesn't matter, except that he's not a cop. He's a fine man, and good to Micky, and..." He waited as she struggled to find the right words. "I need to move on with my life. It's too hard when I see you."

She bowed her head and folded her arms tight against her stomach. When she looked up at him again, her words poured out quickly and pain-filled. "When you're here, I remember too much. I remember Matt too clearly. And you! When Matt was here, the three of us spent a lot of time together, and when he was gone, I thought..." Tears filled her eyes.

"Katie," he whispered.

She shook her head as if to shake off the emotions that gripped her. "I knew there was no chance for me, that you never saw me that way, but I thought if you ever broke up with Angie, that maybe"—she shrugged—"but it's not meant to be. It never was. Now this man, his name is Daniel, he's a good man. My head tells me to give him a chance. But my heart—as long as you're here, I'm stuck in the past. I can't forget Matt. I can't forget you! So, I ask

11

you, please give me time. Give me space."

"I'm sorry, Katie. I had no idea."

"I know!" She stepped closer to him. "You're a good man." She cocked her head, her smile wry. "Obtuse as all get-out, but a good man."

"What will Micky think if I just stop seeing him?"

"He loves you," Katie said. "You'll see him again, and spend time with him again in a few months. But not now." Her tears flowed freely. "Can you understand what I'm saying? Can you forgive me for being so selfish?"

"I understand, Katie."

He turned to leave.

"Paavo." She put her hand on his shoulder, and when he turned around she put her arms around him. She held him tight, as he did her. She cried, and his heart broke for what had been in the past, and would never be again. He held her a long moment, then stepped back.

"Good luck to you, Katie. I hope it works out and you find happiness." He put his hand on her cheek, brushed aside her tears, and then left.

Paavo sat in his car. His hands gripped the wheel, but he didn't start the engine. He should see Angie tonight, but Katie's words were too fresh, too painful. He had no idea that she ever considered such feelings towards him. Obtuse, she had called him. Maybe so.

Now, as much as hearing she wanted to start fresh and find someone else to love heartened him, another part of him cried that it was wrong, that she was Matt's wife and always would be. Matt had been a six-foot-five, two hundred fifty pound lug with a laid-back competence and professionalism that Paavo admired, and a sense of humor that made him a fun guy to be around. How could anyone ever supplant his best friend in her life?

At the same time, he understood completely what she was saying. His visits to her and Micky had kept Matt alive in his mind as well. He had never really gotten over Matt's death. They had been best friends as well as partners, and Paavo had made sure that he never grew that close to his current partner, or to anyone else in Homicide. In a sense, he feared ever again going through the sadness, bitterness, and even guilt that had plagued him after Matt's death. Matt had been alone when he died, and Paavo always felt he should have been with him, been there to protect him, to save him.

Now, he held himself back from others in Homicide. He was a colleague, but little more.

He called Angie and told her something had come up, that he couldn't make it tonight. She sounded disappointed and troubled. She tried to question him, but he had no answers, and soon ended the conversation. The last thing he wanted to do was upset her, but tonight he needed time alone; needed time to think.

Chapter 2

NOT MUCH REMAINED to identify.

The next morning, Paavo and his partner, Toshiro Yoshiwara, stood in an alley in the Financial District, surrounded by high rise offices with restaurants, delis, bars, and a myriad of shops filling the ground floors. The alley mainly existed for garbage pick-up.

They had seen many dead bodies in their time, but none as mangled as the poor sap before them. The brightness of the morning sun, the beauty of a new day, seemed bizarrely at odds with watching the medical examiner's team pull body parts, piece by piece, from a garbage truck. Even hardened crime scene investigators struggled to keep their breakfasts down.

Earlier, one of the scavengers on the route had been wheeling a dumpster back into place when his partner operating the garbage truck told him to climb up to see why it seemed to be straining. The scavenger saw the human legs and feet—jeans and a man's soft leather slip-ons—slowly being sucked into the trash compactor. He screamed for his partner to cut the power, but it was too late. Only one foot had been saved.

Blood dampened the ground in front of the dumpster as well as the metal inside, making it appear as if an altercation had taken place right there, and the victim had been tossed into the dumpster to die.

"We won't be able to tell anything until the medical examiner's team sorts all this out," Paavo said, although from the color, hardness and lividity of the foot that hadn't been smashed, the death had occurred a few days earlier. He tried to find jacket or pants pockets to look for a wallet or other identifying papers, but the material had been badly shredded. At the moment, neither pockets nor their contents were identifiable. Finally, he peered with dismay at the mess that was their crime scene.

Things had been quiet in Homicide before this call came in. Almost too quiet. It had given Paavo time to confirm the decision he had made last night after listening to Katie Kowalski—that Katie had been right. She did need to move on with her life, and so did Micky. And so did he. If she met a good man, one who would be a good husband to her and a father to Micky—a full-time dad, not someone who visited once a month—so much the better for both of them. Paavo would find some way, in time, to continue to be a part of Micky's life, and to be there to make sure the boy was well-treated, safe, and happy. He was good with that.

But now, he turned his full attention to what he knew best, dealing with a murder and the crime scene. It was located in the center of the busiest section of San Francisco during the week, and one of the quietest areas on weekends. The job of canvassing the Financial District and talking to anyone who might have seen or heard something, would be a nightmare.

"The poor bastard's teeth were crushed when his head

went through the compactor," Yosh said. "Dental records won't do it."

Paavo nodded. "Let's hope we have some fingerprints on file."

"Yeah," Yosh said, "once we find his fingers."

Angie and her sister, Caterina Amalfi Swenson, spent five hours going to houses throughout the northern section of San Francisco, Angie's favorite part of the city. Cat, as she liked to call herself, had been an interior designer for many years, and had recently moved to real estate. She was the second oldest of Angie's four sisters, born after Bianca, and before Maria, Francesca, and Angelina, the baby of the family.

Normally, Cat had little to do with her youngest sister, but recently Angie helped her out of a horrific mess in which she was accused of murder. If Angie hadn't dropped everything to go with her to Rome, she didn't know how she would have managed to prove her innocence. Oh, yes...Paavo had helped a bit, too.

She owed Angie, and now Angie was getting payback. Big time. Cat drove with her shoes off because her feet hurt. Louboutin open-toe platform pumps were normally comfortable, but given how far they'd traveled, she was lucky not to ache in more places than her feet.

They had started in the northeast part of the city at Telegraph Hill, and worked their way west through North Beach, Russian Hill, the Marina, Pacific Heights, and now they were in the Presidio Heights area.

The houses went from very expensive to extremely expensive. The one moderately expensive home needed a complete remodel, a new roof, and earthquake retrofitting. A wrecking ball would have been its best solution.

Angie became increasingly depressed. "Let me see what else is on your list," she said, reaching for Cat's realtor listing sheet.

Cat kept hold of the paperwork. "I think you should look for a place outside the city, Angie. How does Paavo feel about the suburbs?"

"I haven't talked to Paavo about any of this yet. I want to see if buying a house is at all feasible for us." She reached again for the sheets.

"The idea of becoming a home-owner seems to have hit you rather suddenly," Cat said, holding the papers in the air as she eyed Angie with suspicion. "Don't you think you should at least talk to Paavo about it before going any further?"

"Why bother him if there's no place we can afford? Like I said, I'd like to see what else is on your list," she repeated.

With what sounded distinctly like a "harrumph," Cat handed Angie the list.

She scanned down the few remaining houses. "Oh, my God!" she cried. "How did you miss this one? It's $600,000 for a house in the Sea Cliff, four bedrooms, two-and-a-half baths, two-car garage, laundry room, tool shed, overlooking the Pacific Ocean. Why didn't we start there? You never even mentioned it! Let's go, quick!"

Cat didn't even look at the listing. "Don't bother."

"What do you mean? It sounds perfect."

"I've heard about that place. It's been listed forever, and has gone pending any number of times, but the deal always falls through."

"How come?"

"I don't know. People find some excuse not to live there, I guess. My office manager told us not to get involved with it. It's a pathway to frustration and a waste of time."

"I want to see it."

"Didn't you hear what I just said?"

"It's my time to waste."

Angie heard a poorly suppressed, "Sheesh."

Chapter 3

HOMICIDE WAS LOCATED on the fourth floor of San Francisco's Hall of Justice building, a massive gray block structure near freeway crossings in the city's South of Market area.

That afternoon, Paavo and Yosh returned to their desks to go over what little information they had turned up so far on the dead body, and to brief the new chief of the Homicide bureau, Lieutenant James Philip Eastwood. Eastwood, however, was in a meeting with the mayor.

Paavo knew they were going to have to wait for information from the medical examiner before they could do much on the case. Right now, the only thing they could say with certainly was that the victim wasn't homeless—he wore shoes and socks far too expensive for that possibility.

Uniformed officers were going door to door asking questions, and one of them might come up with some findings to help them get started.

The phone rang. He expected Lt. Eastwood, but to his surprise, found his fiancée on the line. She almost never called him at work, knowing he didn't like to be disturbed.

"I'm sorry to call," Angie said, "but I've been worried about you. You sounded upset on the phone last night. Is everything all right?"

"Fine."

She waited a moment, then said, "Oh?"

"Really."

"Okay." She didn't sound convinced. "Anyway, I called because I've been thinking about our living arrangements after the wedding. I know you've agreed to move into my apartment, but what if we found a house we could afford to buy? What if I went house-hunting?"

Of all the things he believed she might have been thinking about with their upcoming wedding, their living arrangement afterward wasn't one of them. "House-hunting? Why?"

"I want to make sure that staying in my apartment is right for us," she said.

He wasn't sure whether to be relieved or not. He owned a small bungalow in San Francisco's outer Richmond district. He had gotten it at a decent price because it had no garage, no view, needed work, and was tiny. Angie's shoes couldn't fit in it, let alone the rest of her possessions. She had a much larger apartment, but it was in her father's building. And Salvatore Amalfi didn't like his baby girl marrying a cop. He wanted her to marry a doctor, a lawyer, or—god-forbid—a political up-and-comer. Anyone but a guy who ran around the streets of San Francisco with a gun and a target on his back.

Sal was even unhappier about their relationship since Angie had a propensity for putting herself in danger because of Paavo's cases. "What's this new concern, Angie? Where did it come from?"

"Nowhere," she said.

He didn't believe that one bit.

She continued, "I'm open to change, that's all. This

may be a good time to buy. Do you object?"

"Of course not, if that's what you want to do." The high price of San Francisco property mixed with Angie's expensive taste flashed before his eyes, making him glad debtor's prison was a thing of the past. "But we've got to be able to afford what you find. Us, Angie, not your father."

"Good. I'm here with Cat, and we're going to look at houses. I love you and want you to be happy. You know that don't you?"

"Of course," he said, realizing that since she was with Cat, she had already made up her mind about house-hunting. They soon said their goodbyes.

Paavo shuddered at the thought of Angie and her realtor sister together. They rarely saw eye-to-eye, but when they agreed and put their heads together, anything could happen—including dashing off to Rome, Italy, where they went not long ago and caused one of the more harrowing episodes Paavo had ever experienced.

"What's going on, Paavo?" Yosh asked. "You look worried. Is Angie already spending all your money? You aren't even married yet." Yosh, a six-foot tall Japanese-American, built like a sumo wrestler, had married his first love when in his early twenties.

"She's going house-hunting," Paavo answered.

"I thought your living arrangements were settled."

"Did you say house-hunting?" Bo Benson spun his chair around to face Paavo and then leaned back in it.

"I'm afraid so," Paavo replied.

Bo and Paavo had been the confirmed bachelors of the group. Bo loved women and loved dating. Date many and often was his way of thinking. In his early thirties, smart, good looking, African-American, sharp dresser, he hadn't been tied down yet, and had no plans to be. He liked to joke that Angie had worn Paavo down. Not exactly, but even when Paavo tried to break it off, Angie kept coming around. She was convinced he needed her, and a convinced Angie was a force of nature.

Not that he particularly minded, if truth be told.

"You had a good deal going, moving into Angie's fancy penthouse," Bo said. "Why blow it?"

"Maybe he doesn't want to be her kept man," Luis Calderon chimed in. One marriage, one divorce, and he had been miserable ever since. Calderon, in his late 40's, was sour before the divorce, which many said was the reason the marriage hadn't lasted. After it ended, he made pickles seem sweet. "Moving into her place isn't the best way to start a marriage. Gives the woman too much power. That never works out. You got to show her who's in charge, put her in her place right from day one."

"*Put her in her place?*" Rebecca Mayfield echoed, disgust dripping as she faced Calderon. Rebecca Mayfield, early 30's, had never married. She dated occasionally, but hadn't been serious about anyone as long as Paavo had known her...except maybe him. She and others in the squad often hinted that she was much more 'right' for him than Angelina Amalfi. Tall, blonde, buxom, serious, a crack shot, she was an absolute straight arrow when it came to policy and procedure, and always said exactly what she meant. Quite the opposite was Angie—short, dark hair, with a slight built, she skirted the law or anything else that stood in her way and readily skewed, if not skewered, the truth. All the Amalfis were that way. There was the 'real' world, and then the world according to the Amalfis.

Given all that, Paavo had to admit his cohorts were right. And yet, while Rebecca might be more his type than Angie, she didn't stir his blood, and around her he never did foolish things. He had never met anyone like Angie before, and he couldn't stay away even though that would have been the rational thing to do. But the heart wasn't rational, and his heart was lost to one petite Italian-American who had managed to wrap him around her fancy French-manicured little finger.

Rebecca was still reaming Calderon for his statement. "I'm amazed your marriage lasted as long as it did!" she said. "Just because Angie is willing to give Paavo a little corner of her lavish, expensive apartment which is in a building owned by her father, who has ultimate control over where the couple lives and how they live, and probably what they do and how they spend their money, that doesn't mean Paavo would be 'a kept' anything!"

Paavo looked at Rebecca and winced. He hoped she was joking because if that's what she really thought, he was in trouble.

"Angie basically lives rent free." Yosh teetered on his chair's back legs, hands resting on his protruding stomach. "If Paavo moves in with her and sells his place, think of all the money he'll save. He could invest it, maybe buy his own apartment building in time. In fact, I can't help but wonder when he's going to quit police work to become a real estate magnate. Everyone knows Angie and her father consider his job way too dangerous. Instead of doing this, he can become a property mogul, the 'Donald Trump' of the West Coast."

The others all laughed.

"Can't wait to see his comb-over," Bo chortled.

"Paavo is not going bald!" Rebecca said.

"Not yet," Calderon muttered with a growl. "Just wait until he's married and has all the Amalfi women ordering him around."

The only detective who hadn't said a word during all this was Rebecca's partner, Bill Sutter. He'd been nicknamed 'Never-Take-A-Chance' because he was always super cautious on the job. He'd been thinking about retiring for years and had nightmares that he would be killed a few days before he started collecting his pension. Maybe that was why he hadn't turned in his papers yet.

He looked ready to offer his two cents when, mercifully, Paavo's phone began to ring again. Lt. Eastwood called to say he was ready for the briefing.

Paavo couldn't remember ever being so happy to hear from his boss.

Chapter 4

HERE IT IS," CATERINA said, "51 Clover Lane."
"I can't believe this location." Angie couldn't stop swiveling her head as she took in the view. "It overlooks the Pacific Ocean! This is incredible."

Clover Lane was just off Sea Cliff Avenue on the western edge of San Francisco. The lane contained only two houses--number 51, on the side of the street facing the water, and across from it, number 60, a much smaller home. A guard rail stood at the end of the lane, and beyond it was open space for dog walkers or anyone who might want to scramble down the cliff to the narrow strip of sandy beach below.

The two gray and white clapboard homes appeared surprisingly out-of-place among the mansions that made up the bulk of the Sea Cliff, one of the city's priciest neighborhoods. They seemed all but forgotten out on the small strip of land.

"The house looks a bit dated, don't you think?" Cat stood with one hand on her hip, eying the property. "And there's nothing else here but that little cottage. It looks lonely."

"Lonely? It's surrounded by open space!" Angie eyed

her as if she'd taken leave of her senses. "That's desirable in a city. A little landscaping and fresh paint and it'll look one-hundred percent better. Let's see the inside."

Cat's expression was decidedly sour as she opened the lock box to remove the front door key. Normally, Angie's suspicions would rise at too good of a price for a house, and she would walk away from it. Cat's reluctance to show it to her, however, had the opposite effect.

When Cat opened the door, Angie's thoughts turned from obstinate to ecstatic. The foyer led directly to the living room with a wall of windows.

"The view is breathtaking!" The picture windows faced north to Baker's Beach on the western edge of the Presidio with a glimpse of the Golden Gate Bridge spanning the water to Marin County. Looking west out over the Pacific, she could see the Farallon Islands, for once not lost in fog.

Angie struggled to turn her gaze back to the house. Furniture filled the living room and dining area beside it. "I thought you said no one lived here," Angie said.

"No one is living here," Cat repeated. "The furniture comes with the house. If you don't want it, the seller will move it out before you take possession."

"Well, if I were to take the place, this furniture would all go! It's old and hideous."

As Angie slid open the glass door to the back garden and stepped outside, Caterina's phone chimed news of a text message causing her to dig into her purse to find it. At the same time, the candy dish on the coffee table rose up high in the air and then dropped with a thud onto the area rug.

Angie walked a little way out onto the patio. The yard had a level area, and then sloped downward. A surrounding fence gave protection from the area's namesake, the sea cliff.

"It's a client," Cat said as she composed a reply. "Give me a moment before we see the rest of the house, okay?" Cat hit "send" and then looked up. "Angie?" Finally, she stuck her head outside. "What are you doing? I thought I heard you come back inside. I've been in here talking to myself!"

"Just looking around." Angie went back indoors.

"That yard will never do once you have kids," Cat said, pulling the sliding glass door shut. "They'd be over that fence and playing on the cliff in no time at all."

"You may be right," Angie said. "But by the time Paavo and I have kids old enough to go outside and play without being watched, I suspect we'll do like so many people and move out of San Francisco. While we're newlyweds, however, I plan to enjoy city life. Let's see the kitchen."

They walked through the dining area which also had a wall of windows facing the ocean, to the kitchen. The wall between the kitchen and dining room had been removed. The bar and stools in its place gave the kitchen an open and airy feel.

"This kitchen is a nightmare," Cat said, running her hand over the off-white porcelain tile countertops. The appliances were also white. "I'd need sunglasses to work in here."

The refrigerator door suddenly swung open. Then, the oven door did the same.

"My God, these appliances really are old," Angie said as she shut both doors. "Or they were badly mishandled by someone. Not that it matters. I would want new, top-of-the-line appliances and granite countertops wherever I lived. This kitchen could be made truly beautiful!"

The refrigerator door opened once more and she gave

it a shove with her elbow, closing it as she moved out of the kitchen. The more she saw of the house, the less sense it made that it hadn't sold, and that the owners weren't asking twice as much for it.

On the opposite side of the living room, a large master bedroom and bath also faced the water. One small room, perfect for a den or a future nursery, was across the hall from it, along with a guest powder room. Upstairs were two more bedrooms and a full bathroom. The view from the upstairs bedrooms was even more breath-taking than on the main level. Angie could see making one a guest room and the letting Paavo have the other to use as an office, man-cave, or whatever he wanted.

Angie was beside herself at this find. "If Paavo and I were to buy this house," she said, "Paavo could either sell his house or rent it out and put the rent money towards the mortgage. We could make this work, you know." She glanced at her sister. "By the way, your perfume is awfully strong. I noticed it when I came downstairs."

"Strong? It's the same as always!" Cat said indignantly. "But I think you've gotten ahead of yourself. There are better houses out there than this one."

"But none with a better view or price!" Angie went off to see the laundry room, mudroom and garage. Cat stayed in the living room and made a quick phone call back to her office manager.

"I think I'm falling in love," Angie said as she rejoined her sister.

Cat had just ended the call, dropped the phone back into her handbag and faced Angie with a big smile. "If you really want to buy the place, I'm sure I could get a good deal for you. I still owe you for that little incident that sent us to Italy. I'll even throw in my share of the commission.

Call it a wedding present for you and Paavo."

"Really? That's awfully generous." Angie just stared at her, wondering what was up. Familial love didn't flow in Cat's veins; money did.

"Nothing's too good for my baby sister."

Now, Angie felt certain something odd was going on, but she was too excited to care. She spotted the candy dish on the floor. "Funny, I hadn't noticed that before," she said as she picked it up and put it back where it belonged. "This house could be the one!"

"You'll have to get Paavo out here right away," Cat advised. "Why don't you call him and see when he's available?"

Angie grew even more suspicious of her sister's about face. "Wait, let me think about this first," she said. "The problem is, it's too perfect...except for this hideous furniture. It's been on the market a long time, so why hasn't it sold? I'd like to know more before I get Paavo involved. Could you find out its history? You said others dropped out of the deal. I'd like to know why."

"What does it matter what others did if you love it?" Cat asked, with an emphasis on the word 'love.'

Cat's words and demeanor troubled Angie. "I'm not going to think about buying a place that has some kind of bad karma or mystery attached to it." Her tone was emphatic and determined. "Find out all you can. Also, I want Connie to see it and hear its story. Only if everything sounds good will I bring Paavo out here."

"Connie? You're kidding me!" Cat shuddered.

"Connie has a clear head. She'll be perfect."

"Whatever," Cat muttered as they went out the door.

As they walked out to Cat's car, they missed what seemed to be an act of ceramic suicide as the candy dish rose off the table, flew through the air, hit the stonework around the fireplace and landed in tiny pieces on the hearth.

Evelyn Ramirez, the Medical Examiner, called Paavo to her office. It was in the basement, along with the city morgue and the autopsy room.

"I haven't had a chance to do the autopsy yet," she said, "but I found something that might help identify the victim, or at least give you a clue to someone who knows him."

She picked up an evidence bag with a piece of a business card inside it. "It was covered in blood and stuck to some clothing. I suspect that's why whoever removed everything else missed this. I used a wash to remove as much of the blood as I could. In any case, I did some investigating of my own with the help of a phone book." The book lay open behind her desk and she pointed to an advertisement in it as she spoke. "The card looks like it's from Zygog Software in South San Francisco. You can see that the 'Zyg' and the logo match Zygog's. I'm not sure of the name on the card, but it looks like 'Tay' something. The rest of the card hasn't been found yet."

"Good job," Paavo said. "This gives us a start. The fingerprints, such as they were, got us nowhere."

Paavo and Yosh immediately drove to Zygog and asked to speak to the head of the personnel department. They explained the situation, leaving out most of the gorier details, and showed him a photo of the business card.

"That's our card, all right," Larry Peters said. "Tay...hmm. We have a Taylor Bedford who's our top salesmen. Let's hope it's not him. But your victim could easily be one of his clients. Let's see if Taylor's available to speak with you." Peters picked up the office phone and punched in a number.

He looked pale as he hung up and faced he detectives. "The staff secretary said he hasn't arrived yet. He is expected; he should have been here by now."

Paavo glanced at Yosh, then said, "May we see his boss?"

"Certainly." Peters led them to Mark Carter's office and quickly explained the situation.

"Let's hope Taylor is all right," Carter said. He was in his fifties, slim, with glasses and a receding hairline.

"Would you describe Bedford to us?" Paavo asked.

"He's a bit over six feet, good physique—probably goes to the gym while he travels to stay fit. Brown hair; brown eyes."

"Age?" Paavo asked.

"Forty."

"Distinguishing marks or anything about him that might help with identification?"

"Nothing I know of," Carter said.

The description fit that of their victim, as best they and the M.E. could tell.

"Would you like me to call his home?" Carter asked. "He should have returned on Friday. Maybe he's simply sick."

Paavo and Yosh listened as Carter talked to Larina Bedford. She said she expected Taylor home last night but he hadn't made it. She had thought about calling Carter to ask him where Taylor might be, but decided to wait a little longer.

"I can't imagine what happened to him," Carter said to Mrs. Bedford. "But on the road things sometimes do get screwed-up. I'll let you know as soon as I hear from him."

With that he hung up and faced the detectives. "This doesn't look good at all."

"No, it doesn't," Paavo agreed. He and Yosh wrote down Taylor Bedford's home address and phone number, plus other identifying information.

"Before we go," Paavo said to Carter, "what's Taylor Bedford's position here?"

"Sales. Our company produces one-stop software that helps tool and die manufacturers and sales companies inventory and price their equipment, send bills, and so on. It also provides software assistance to mechanical engineers who work closely with the tool and die makers. Taylor's territory is northern California. He travels two weeks a month to visit clients and find new ones."

"How easy is it to learn to sell such software?" Yosh asked.

"Not easy at all. It's a rarified world. That's why Taylor has a huge territory and travels so much. He's our most dedicated salesmen. I have to believe he's all right."

Chapter 5

CONNIE ROGERS LOCKED up her gift shop, Everyone's Fancy, at six o'clock on the nose and followed the directions Angie gave her to Clover Lane. She arrived twenty minutes later.

As usual, she was on time; Angie was not. Connie and Angie met when Paavo investigated the murder of her sister, Tiffany, some time back. They immediately hit it off and had been close friends ever since. She once heard Angie's oldest sister refer to her as "Ethel" to Angie's "Lucy," which she found insulting to both of them...most of the time.

Ten minutes later, Angie's silver Mercedes CL600 coupe pulled into the driveway next to Connie's ancient red Toyota Corolla. Cat's white BMW SUV right parked behind her. "Thank you so much for meeting us," Angie said to Connie as she got out of her car.

"I'm glad to help. From the outside it looks promising," Connie said. "Great neighborhood."

"We'll go in and look around. Cat's still trying to find out the history of the place. As soon as she does, she'll tell me everything she's learned."

Cat walked up to them. "I'll let you two in, but then I've got to run. It's a long drive to Tiburon, and I want to get home before dark. Now, Angie, I'm trusting you to lock up the place before you leave. You know how important it is to me that you don't mess up anything if I give you this key."

"I know, I know. I'm not a child!" Angie wondered when her big sister would stop treating her like an idiot. "But first, have you found out anything at all yet?"

"Not much," Cat said. "The owner is a widow. Apparently, she used to live in the house, but after her husband died she moved out and it became a rental. Now, her daughter put the house up for sale. I suppose the owner is too old to handle her affairs anymore."

"Well, that makes sense," Angie said. "But it doesn't tell me why it's so cheap and hasn't sold in...how long has it been on the market?"

"Two years. But the real estate market has been soft."

"Not in San Francisco." Angie glanced down the lane to Sea Cliff Avenue. "And especially not in this neighborhood."

Cat had no answer.

"All right, let's go inside," Angie said.

Cat opened the lockbox, and removed the key. "I could just unlock the door, and then put the key back in this box." Cat gave Angie a stern look. "But in case you two lock yourself out of the house by mistake, or find some other door that needs to be unlocked with the key, I'm going to trust you with it."

"All right, already!" Angie found all her older sisters very exasperating at times.

Cat showed her how to relock the box after placing the key back inside. She then left.

"Are you sure you want my opinion?" Connie asked as Angie unlocked the door. "If you love the house, what does it matter what I think?"

"I value your opinion," Angie said. "Also, I want to see it without Cat standing over me. She's acting very strange about this place. One minute she says I don't want it, and the next she's practically insisting I buy it. Something's going on with her, and I don't know what it is."

"What worries me," Connie said, "is that the house was a rental, and now has sat empty for a couple of years. Clearly, there's something wrong with it. The land alone is worth what they're asking. You and Cat both know that, Angie. I'll look at it, but you need to as well, and not in a starry-eyed way."

"I'm never starry-eyed," Angie said. "Although this place is a quite a steal. Let's go in."

She opened the front door, and Connie's immediate reaction was everything Angie had hoped for. The view was even more breath-taking now than it had been earlier because the sunset over the ocean had turned the sky a cascade of red and orange.

"Oh no, what's this?" Angie hurried to the broken candy dish on the fireplace hearth. "This wasn't here earlier. It must mean somebody else has come to see the house! Somebody else might be interested! Someone might even make an offer on it before I get a chance!"

"Calm down. It's been empty for a couple of years; it won't sell overnight," Connie said as she wandered into the kitchen, then stuck her head into the garage before heading towards the opposite side of the house to see the bedrooms and bathrooms.

"What do you think?" Angie asked hopefully.

"It's a beautiful house, but..." Connie put her hands on

her hips and looked around. "I don't know. This whole place has a strange vibe, as if someone is still living here. It feels as if the owner could come walking through that door any second and demand we leave."

"Well, that's not going to happen," Angie said.

Connie wouldn't let it go. "I wonder why the owner isn't still using it as a rental. Why leave it empty for two years? And what's with all the furniture?"

"You've made your point." Angie folded her arms. She had thought much the same thing, but hearing Connie voice the concerns didn't make her happy.

Connie still wasn't through. "Keeping the house meant the owner dusted, vacuumed, did yard work, and paid taxes on it. That's crazy. I believe if something is too good to be true, run. This deal is definitely too good to be true."

Angie cringed. "Don't you trust my sister?" she demanded. The question sounded lame even to her.

"I trust you," Connie said. To her, Caterina and Angie were mirror images. While Angie was remarkably selfless when she wasn't in monomaniacal one-track-mind mode such as with this house, Cat was completely, unabashedly selfish. When both were on the same wave length, heaven help anyone standing in their way. In fact, all five of the Amalfi sisters were that way.

Behind them, a vase with silk flowers rose up, suspended in mid-air, from the small round table it decorated.

"The house does seem perfect," Connie admitted. "And it also seems you've made up your mind about it, no matter what I say."

"I'm sorry," Angie said, realizing she ran roughshod over her friend's opinion. "You're right that I'm looking at it purely emotionally. I need your clear-headed thinking.

What am I overlooking?"

Connie folded her arms and walked around. "I don't know. Rationally, it's great. It's got a fantastic location. How many homes in San Francisco aren't squeezed between two others? Your neighbor sneezes and you shout 'Gesundheit!' It's a nice size; it's pretty and well built. You'll get a home inspection so you'll know if it needs a new roof, or new electrical wiring, and so forth. There's nothing I can rationally object to."

The vase floated across the room towards the stone fireplace.

"But...?"

Connie shrugged. "Maybe it's the thought of all the hours you'll have to spend here alone at night, waiting for Paavo because he's off on some homicide case until all hours. But I suppose if the case is interesting you'll be sticking your oars in the water as usual, so being alone out here won't be happening."

The vase stopped moving.

"Stick my 'oars in the water'? What's that supposed to mean?" Angie asked, hands on hips. "I'll admit that sometimes his homicide cases are interesting, but I've never, ever, gotten involved where I'm not wanted or, should I say, not needed."

The vase did an about face and headed back towards the table.

Angie turned her head ever so slightly...and jumped.

"What's wrong?" Connie asked, startled.

Angie gawked as the vase slowly settled onto the edge of the round table, and then slid to its center. She blinked several times. "Uh..."

"Angie?"

She walked over to the vase, stared at it a long

moment. "Nothing."

Connie put her hand to her chin as she continued to look around the room. "All right. If you must know, what bothers me about this house is what I already said: I can't get over the feeling that someone is still living here."

Angie turned her back on the vase, then looked over her shoulder at it once more. "You're giving me the creeps!" Clearly, her eyes had been playing tricks on her. "And you're making me see things. So just stop it!"

Connie placed her hand on the glossy white woodwork framing the opening to the kitchen. "If walls could talk, I wonder what these walls would say."

Angie shuddered. "The more you talk, the more I don't want to know! Cat suggested that the past is best left in the past."

"Well, if Cat suggested it, how can it possibly be wrong?" Connie said. Angie knew she was being sarcastic. "Why not just see what Paavo thinks? If he hates it, case closed. If he likes it, you can always investigate further if you want to."

"That's a great idea!" Angie nearly jumped for joy. "No reason I should put all this on my shoulders! Paavo should have a say. Now, before we go, I'll clean up the pieces of this broken candy dish. I'm going to buy a replacement. If I tell Cat the dish broke, she'll find some way to blame it on me!"

She picked up the pieces. The bottom of the dish bore an imprint of English Spode china, Garden Rose pattern. "I know a shop downtown where I can get a replacement, or something close to it," Angie said. "Cat will never know."

"I'll leave that to you, Angie," Connie said as Angie switched off the lights and locked the front door.

oOo

Paavo and Yosh took Taylor Bedford's coffee cup from his office and brought it to the crime lab where they matched the prints on the cup with those of the corpse in the autopsy room.

Now, they rang the doorbell of the dead man's house. Judging from its size and its Marina district location, the Zygog sales job paid a lot more than Paavo would have expected.

A strikingly beautiful woman with sparkling blue eyes and black hair opened the door. "Are you Larina Bedford?" Paavo asked, showing his badge. Yosh did the same.

Her blue eyes widened with fear. "Is this about my husband?"

"We would like to speak to you," Yosh said.

She invited them into the living room and they had her sit while they told her as gently as possible that her husband had been killed.

"Do you need me to identify his body?" she asked. Her eyes misted, but no tears fell.

"It won't be...possible," Yosh said, struggling to find a better word and realizing he couldn't.

She looked ill. "My God," she whispered.

They asked if they could call someone to be with her during this time.

"No, Inspectors." She turned her head away from their scrutiny. "I'm used to being alone." She took a few deep breaths then faced them again. "I knew something was wrong when Taylor didn't come home last night. He always comes home Sunday night. I tried to call several times, but his phone went to voice mail. I hoped he had been delayed on his return trip and that's why he wasn't here, but that didn't explain why he hadn't phoned to tell me. He was"— her voice broke—"a thoughtful man."

"How long had he been away?" Paavo asked.

"Two weeks, as usual. He traveled for business. Two weeks away; two weeks home. That was his schedule." She stepped into the kitchen for a box of Kleenex. Taking one, she lightly dabbed the corners of her eyes.

"When did you last speak to him?" Paavo asked.

"Friday."

"Where was he?"

"Sacramento, I think. I'm not sure. He has, had, a lot of customers there."

That didn't make sense to Paavo. Sacramento was only two hours from San Francisco. Why wasn't he home sooner? "Did he work weekends?"

"In a sense, he did. He called it 'schmooze' time. He believed a customer found it hard to transfer his business to a competitor after being wined and dined. So he'd usually set up golf games or other outings for his clients on weekends."

"And you didn't expect him home until Sunday night?" Paavo asked. "Was that his usual day to come home?"

"Yes. He would roll in about nine p.m. We'd talk, and then he headed to bed to be bright eyed Monday morning. He was usually exhausted when he got home."

"Do you have the names of the customers or places where he golfed?" Paavo asked. "Or who he met with over the weekend?"

She shook her head. "I'm sorry. I know it sounds odd, but he traveled so much, I stopped trying to keep up with him years ago. His secretary should know."

"What's her name?" Yosh asked.

"His name is Otto. Otto Link."

Chapter 6

YOU WON'T HAVE TO worry about a thing, my dear,"
Diane LaGrande said even before she sat down on
Angie's sofa. She insisted on visiting her clients' homes to
get a sense of their taste and color choices. That sounded
logical to Angie, and she invited her over. "I've done this
many, many times. I know exactly what is needed for a
magnificent wedding."

"I'm glad to hear that," Angie said. After her unhappy
experience with a wedding planner her sister Frannie had
praised—she should have known better than to trust
Frannie!—she decided to go with the one constantly
written up in the *San Francisco Chronicle's* style section as
the best in the Bay Area, and who charged accordingly. But
this was Angie's one and only wedding, and in such things,
price should be no object.

"Is this your first marriage?" Diane asked.

"Yes, it is." Since it was morning, Angie served mimosa
with miniature cinnamon rolls and strawberry tarts.

"Isn't that precious!" Diane took a big gulp of the
champagne and orange mixture, then folded one leg over
the other, and looked around the apartment, evidently

secure in the idea that Angie could afford her service. "We'll definitely create a wedding suitable to someone who lives in an apartment like this." She flashed a big smile as she took in Angie's art and furniture. Her gaze zeroed in on one wall. "Oh, my!" She stood and walked towards it. "Is that a Cezanne? A real Cezanne?"

"Yes," Angie said. It was a small lithograph.

"He's one of my favorites. An inspiration to me. Ah, yes! I can see it now." Diane threw back her head, waving her arms as if painting a tableau. "You! Dressed in reds and yellows and greens; colors rich yet delicate like this Cezanne. Your bridesmaids in a dotted impressionist array... *quel magnifique!*"

"I want a white dress," Angie said, folding her hands on her lap.

Diane slowly lowered her chin, eyes open and piercing. "White?" she asked in a voice that sounded like she'd just described the inside of a dirty toilet. "Oh, that's right. You're a new bride. Oh, well, I'm sure *you* can wear white, but we'll have your bridesmaids in beautiful color! And never mind your dress." She fluttered her hands as if dismissing Angie completely. "Everything else is what's important. We'll make your wedding into a veritable rainbow of colors, with an emphasis on the deeper, richer hues. Purple, blue...*indigo!*"

"I'm not really an indigo person," Angie said.

Diane lifted one eyebrow. "So?"

Angie cleared her throat. "Well, I am the bride."

"Yes. The bride who will be wearing white." Diane looked down on her with something that struck Angie as very much akin to pity. "As I said, my dear, I've done this many times. Many times! My weddings are creative treasures. The very best possible! Memorable! Colorful!

Daring!" She picked up her purse and turned towards the door. "I've got a good idea of what you want. I'll get started on it right away. I may need to borrow the Cezanne at some point, to get the colors right."

"Wait!" Angie hurried after her. "Let me think about this. I've got more interviews coming."

"Excuse me?" Diane looked down on Angie as if she had two heads. "I told you I was free to work on your wedding. Surely, there isn't anyone else you could possibly want."

Angie squared her shoulders. "I expect you're right, but I haven't yet made my choice."

Diane sniffed. "Well, I hope I'm still available when you come crawling back. Be sure to call me as soon as you decide, or I may have to disappoint."

"I couldn't have that," Angie said, trying not to sound too sarcastic.

"I should hope not." With that, Diane left.

Angie no sooner got rid of Ms. LaGrande than Cat unexpectedly showed up at her door. She stormed into the apartment then swirled around to face Angie. "You want Connie to be your realtor, fine! Let her handle the house sale!" Cat loudly harrumphed.

"Relax, Cat!" Angie went into the kitchen to make her a mimosa. She had plenty remaining. "This has nothing to do with Connie. The questions are mine, and I'm sure Paavo, too, will want to know the answers. Why did the owner stop renting out the house, and what happened that caused others not to buy it? They're simple questions and should have simple answers."

Cat took off her coat, then walked to the kitchen doorway, arms folded. "Who cares as long as you like the place? Are the answers really that important?"

Angie looked Cat straight in the eye as she held out the drink. "Yes!"

Cat heaved a sigh and gave a disgusted shake of the head. She took the drink to the sofa, then perched on the edge of it. "All right, if you must know. For a long time, when home prices were doing nothing but going up, the house was considered the owner's nest egg. Now, times have changed. That's all." She reached for a cinnamon roll and took a big bite.

Angie sat in a chair, interested in hearing all Cat had learned. "That doesn't answer my question. Why didn't it sell?"

Cat put the roll down, professed it delicious, then took a couple of sips of her drink before explaining. "The house did sell...several times. But the people who bought it backed out before the sale was finalized. It happens all the time."

Angie scooted forward. "Do you mean they changed their minds and backed out? All of them? That doesn't make sense!"

"Calm down. It's nothing. They had reasons that had nothing to do with the house."

Angie folded her arms, her gaze shooting daggers at her sister. "Such as?"

Cat drank some more, then put the glass on a coaster on the coffee table. "One realized she had acrophobia, and couldn't stand being so close to a drop off. Although it's called a cliff, it's not a sheer drop. People can, and do, climb on it all the time. Anyway, another said the constant sound of the waves made her nervous. You know that most people love to hear the sound of waves, and find it soothing and relaxing and oh, so very—"

"Is that all?" Angie interrupted.

"Well, let me see." Cat picked up the glass again, taking a big gulp of the champagne-orange juice mix this time. "There was the couple who got a divorce. Luckily their marriage fell apart before they signed the final papers."

"Great luck," Angie muttered sarcastically. Cat didn't even notice. Angie's brows crossed. "Any more?"

Cat cleared her throat. "Well...I mustn't leave out the woman who had a, uh, nervous breakdown before signing papers. The bank denied her loan at that point, so she shouldn't really count."

"Okay, I guess. That would certainly tie the place up for months with each transaction. But that doesn't answer my other question. Why didn't they continue to rent the house?"

"You know renters, they mess up places. The owner wanted it to look nice to sell it."

"For two years?"

"Maybe...maybe no one wanted to rent it for a while."

"Why not?"

"I don't know." Her voice dropped. "*Maybebecausethefirstrentersdied.*"

"What was that? Did you mumble..."

"Who cares what happened!" Cat said loudly. She began eating the rest of her cinnamon roll, saying a few words between bites. "None of it matters if you like the house. Just get Paavo to see it. If you buy it, I'm sure you'll both be happy as clams."

Angie looked at her suspiciously. "Who said clams are happy? What else was it you said? Something about first renters?"

Cat finished the roll and then knocked back the rest of her mimosa. "I've no idea what you're talking about," she said innocently. "Now, let's think about something else. How are your wedding plans coming along?"

"*Maybe because the first renters...?*" Angie tried to recall...then, she felt herself go cold, as if all the blood drained from her body. She jumped to her feet. "*Died!* That's what you said, wasn't it? 'Maybe because the first renters died.' What's that supposed to mean? Are you telling me a couple died while renting the house?!"

"They...apparently, they died while living in the house. But it happened years and years ago."

"What!"

"Don't worry! They didn't die inside the house." Cat sounded indignant. "California law says I must disclose it if anyone died *inside* the house, for pity's sake!"

"Well, that's good!"

"Realtors have rules, you know. And a murder must be disclosed."

"A murder? They were *murdered?*" Angie shrieked. "Where?"

Cat swallowed. "Out on the cliff. They were found near the edge of the cliff, both shot to death. But it's not even part of this property, it's beyond it. And it happened before the owner put up the fence."

"Oh, my God! A murder!"

"It's nothing to worry about. Besides, it happened years and years ago."

"How many years ago?"

"The early 1980's I believe."

"What? The 1980's? Wait a minute. I thought you said the house has been empty since those renters...well, since they died. Did I misunderstand?"

"Not exactly."

"Didn't you say the house has been empty two years?"

"I said it's been for sale for two years."

"And it's been empty...?"

"Thirty...plus."

Angie said nothing for a long while, then sat back down and slowly and calmly asked, "Are you saying no one has lived in the house since renters were murdered there over thirty years ago?"

"Look on the bright side." Cat gave her a big smile. "The place is practically new! It hasn't been worn at all."

"Ah ha!" Angie cried. "So, you're trying to push some loser house off on me!"

"It's not a loser house! It's a lovely house that has simply had bad luck. And I never tried to push it off on you! You're the one who insisted you see it while I told you to ignore it, that it's had a troubled past. But *nooooo!* You had to see it! You can't blame the house for that! Or me!" Cat stood and poked Angie in the shoulder with her forefinger. "You, of all people, should understand bad luck. Think of all the jobs you've tried, and haven't gotten anywhere with. You've been a food columnist, did radio, television, ran a cake baking business, tried to become a chocolatier—"

Angie pushed her hand away to stop the obnoxious jabbing of her shoulder. Even as a kid, Cat had skinny, pointy, fingers of steel and used them with relish. "All right, all right! I get the message." Memories of all those jobs...and others...rushed at her in a wave of failure.

"Just as no one can blame you for the problems with your jobs," Cat preached, "so you can't blame the house just because the right person hasn't bought it yet. Maybe you and Paavo are the right people. You should be sympathetic towards it!"

Angie seethed. "If I thought the house had feelings,

maybe I would be!"

"But yesterday you loved the place. Why should this matter?"

"Apparently, it mattered to all the others who wanted to buy it!"

Cat looked stricken, then laughed, a bit too loudly. "Silly girl. When can Paavo see it?"

So far, Paavo had not found a reason for anyone to want Taylor Bedford dead, yet nothing about the case felt as if it were a random murder. The M.E. had placed the time of death as sometime Saturday evening, when Larina Bedford said Taylor should have been in Sacramento with some clients. Something told Paavo that he and Yosh were going to be spending a lot of time tracking down out of town clients and at the company's headquarters.

After long hours with nothing to show for them, the two detectives decided it would be best to go home and start again fresh in the morning.

Home for Paavo didn't mean going to his small house, but being with Angie. He called and asked her out to dinner to make up for missing dinner with her two nights in a row, but she insisted on cooking for him so he could relax. He liked that since she cooked better than any restaurant he knew of. She planned some "Italian comfort food"—*spaghetti carbonara* with homemade bread, red wine, and a garden salad with a variety of green vegetables, tomato, cucumber, and avocado.

He knocked on the door and she opened it almost immediately.

Even after getting to know her better than any other person in his life, the beauty and warmth of her smile when she greeted him still awed him. He liked nothing more than to look into her wide-set brown eyes as he put his arms around her and kissed her. After a while, he took off his jacket, removed his shoulder holster and gun and left them on a table in the corner of the living room while she poured him a beer, his beverage of choice, and a glass of chardonnay for herself.

He loosened his tie as he settled his long body on the sofa. She put Miles Davis on the stereo since Paavo liked jazz, then sat down beside him. He put an arm around her.

"Tell me about your house-hunting adventures," he said. "Did Cat come up with any places you like?"

Angie nestled her head on his shoulder. "She did do that. The problem with most places is the price. Most houses in neighborhoods I like are outrageously expensive. Unless my job prospects change, we can't begin to consider them."

The last thing Paavo wanted was to have Angie talking about her job prospects, or lack of them. To him, she was bright, clever, and talented, and had a knack for cooking right up there—to his palette—with chefs in the fancy restaurants she sometimes dragged him to. He felt sure she could be another Wolfgang Puck, Emeril, or any of the numerous big-time chefs she talked about. But for whatever reason, that ability had never led to a good job.

"I don't want you to feel you have to work, Angie. If the wolf is at the door, that's one thing, but let's not start out married life with that kind of burden. We'll simply wait until the right place in the right neighborhood comes on the market."

More than most people, homicide detectives knew San Francisco wasn't all quaint cable cars and popular tourist attractions. Like any big city, there were areas that weren't safe during the day, and became hell holes at night.

Innocent people died or were maimed simply because they were caught in the cross-fire. He'd never forgive himself if he did anything that put Angie in danger--especially when she did that so well by herself.

"Actually," she said, sitting upright. "I did find one house that I like, that's in a great neighborhood and is affordable."

"Oh?" It wasn't like her not to blurt out good news. "What's wrong with it?"

"Why would you think that?"

"Nothing." He lied. "Tell me about it."

"Right now, I'm still checking it out. The house has been on the market for a couple of years. It's a lovely place in the Sea Cliff, with an unobstructed view of the Pacific Ocean."

"The Sea Cliff? You mean the area where, not long ago, your sister tried to sell a house and found a dead body inside?"

"Yes, Cat knows the area extremely well." Angie didn't seem to realize what was wrong with this picture.

Paavo shook his head. "Those places cost a million plus. What are you thinking? You know that's out of our reach no matter how generous your father will be with the loan terms. Sometimes I wonder if it's a good idea to get involved in a house at this point in our lives."

"Don't worry so," she said, giving him a quick kiss. "What if I told you the house was listed for $600,000? It's a lot of money, but not for San Francisco, and not for that area."

The unbelievable price stunned Paavo. His little cottage would sell for between $400,000 to $500,000 not because of the house but because of the value of the land it sat on. "As I asked earlier, what's wrong with it?"

She grabbed his hand. "Do you think it's a good deal if everything checks out?"

"Check it out really carefully," he cautioned.

"Wonderful!" She gave him a big hug. Finally, he saw the Angie he knew and loved as she bubbled over with enthusiasm. He was about to kiss her when she popped her head up. "As soon as my questions get answered, I'll take you to see the place. I hope, I hope, I hope it all turns out as I—"

"Hope?" he offered.

"Yes!" She threw her arms around his neck and kissed him. He tried to hold her, but she sat up again. "Now, before we have dinner and can talk about other things, there's one little bit of information you can help me with."

"Oh?"

"The last couple who lived there were murdered...not in the house, but behind it, on the cliff above China Beach. It happened sometime in the 1980s. Would you be able to find out who they were and why they were killed?"

"We should have some sort of record," he said. "But that was over thirty years ago. You don't think that's why the house's price is so low, do you?"

"Definitely," she said. "If a murder happened in the house, I wouldn't want anything to do with it."

Now he sat upright. "Really? If it's a good deal, who cares what took place thirty years ago?"

"I'd want to know!"

"Afraid of bad juju? Ghosts?" he asked with a grin. "It's a house. Walls, window, doors. What people have or haven't done near the house means nothing."

"You are so logical, Paavo," she said. "What would I do without you? Are you saying if we both like the house and everything else about it seems fine, maybe we'll want to buy it?"

"That's right."

"Interesting," she exclaimed. "And sensible. Okay, I feel much better now! And I'll be even better when you find out what happened out there, who the people were that were murdered, and why. Cat assures me the murders had nothing to do with the house."

She was protesting too much. It troubled him. Sensible and logical were not usually part of Angie's vocabulary. "Look," he said, "if you would be bothered by what happened—"

"No, no, no! I can put it out of my mind. Whatever happened to them won't have anything to do with how I feel about buying the property. It's simply idle curiosity."

He had dealt with those "idle curiosity" requests of Angie's before, and pretty much reached the conclusion that as long as what she wanted to know wasn't illegal, it saved time to simply comply rather than have her wear him down bit by bit. "Give me the address and anything else you might have, and I'll see what I can find out."

"Wonderful!" She stood up. "Dinner will be ready in a little while!"

He caught her hand and drew her back down to his side. "I've missed you," he said softly as he took her into his arms. "Would it be so bad to start with dessert?"

Chapter 7

WHEN PAAVO LEFT FOR work the next morning, Angie woke up long enough for him to kiss her good-bye, and he was pretty sure she had gone back to sleep before he left her apartment. Since their engagement, he had moved some clothes, toiletries and shaving supplies to her house. He could imagine living here. It was convenient, it was a beautiful place, the rent Angie paid was miniscule...but it wasn't his and wasn't hers. She had been right about that. If she found a good house at the right price, personally, he wouldn't care if the Manson family had lived there. But he could see that Angie might.

In Homicide, he went through Taylor Bedford's appointment book and credit card expenditures. It showed that he had been at the Masco Tool and Supply in Sacramento on the Friday before his death.

Strangely, Bedford's credit card didn't show any hotel charges for Friday or Saturday nights. Although Bedford had been killed on Saturday, he wasn't expected home until Sunday, so he should have been staying somewhere those two nights...unless Larina Bedford lied, and Bedford had, in fact, come home after his last meeting in Sacramento.

Paavo looked over several months of credit card charges and a clear pattern emerged. For one week, Monday through Thursday, there would be a string of hotel bills throughout northern California, then a three night stay at the Mountain Shadows Resort in Healdsburg, followed by another string of Monday through Thursday hotel bills all over the area. For the next two weeks, there would be no hotel charges. This agreed with what Larina Bedford said about Taylor being home two weeks, and then two weeks on the road.

But she also said he spent weekends with clients. No charges were put on his business credit card for those expenses, however—except for the weekends in Healdsburg. Paavo would need to check Bedford's personal credit cards to see if he covered all those expenses himself.

Now, while Yosh went back to Zygog Software to continue discussions with Bedford's boss, secretary, and co-workers, Paavo decided to head north.

Sacramento was about two hours from San Francisco. It should have taken longer to drive there, but anyone who stuck to the 65 mile per hour speed limit along the multilane Highway 80 would get run over by every other car on the road. Slow drivers, not speeders, were the cause of road rage on California highways.

Talking to the owner of Masco, Paavo learned that Bedford had spent only two hours with him on Friday morning going over updates and add-ons to the software packages, plus arranging for a trainer to come in and give some advanced lessons to the accounting staff. Paavo asked other key people if they had any dealings with Bedford on Friday. None had, and the owner had never been taken out to dinner or anywhere else by Bedford in all the time they had worked together. And, he didn't even play golf.

So, if Bedford didn't spent time with his client on Friday evening or Saturday, where had he gone?

Paavo had photocopied a number of other pages from Bedford's appointment book and decided to check on some other clients near Sacramento. None of them had seen Bedford for over a month. None ever went to dinner, golf games, or anything else with the salesman.

Going through Bedford's business charges, he spent Monday night in Redding, Tuesday in Shasta, Wednesday in Marysville, and Thursday in Sacramento.

Before that, he had spent the weekend in Healdsburg...Friday, Saturday, and Sunday nights, just as he had every fourth week for the five months' worth of statements Paavo had copied. Why there? The small town in northern Sonoma County was hardly a hotbed of anything, let alone the tool and die trade.

Bedford had only one client in Healdsburg, Steelhead Tool and Die.

Paavo drove to Healdsburg where he met with the owner of Steelhead, a small family-run business. He learned Bedford showed up on that Friday afternoon for no more than twenty or so minutes to check on how things were going. He did that like clockwork, about once a month. While the owner appreciated the attention, he hadn't asked for it and frankly rarely needed it. As with the Sacramento client, the owner had never gone to dinner or attended any kind of social outing with Bedford.

Paavo saw a pattern. He saved himself some travel by phoning Bedford's clients in Ukiah, Eureka and Shasta. Same story in all three places. Bedford was not the winer-and-diner his wife thought.

While in Healdsburg, he went to the Mountain Shadows Resort, where Bedford booked rooms every fourth Friday, Saturday, and Sunday nights.

"Oh, yes, I know Mr. Bedford," the desk clerk said solemnly, his black eyes wide as he looked from Paavo's badge to the stern detective.

"He's a regular guest here, I understand. Once every month or so, he stayed the entire weekend," Paavo said.

"Well, um." The clerk cleared his throat. "I'm not sure you could say that. He comes here once every four weeks, and he always pays for three nights. But"—*cough, cough*—"he doesn't stay the whole time. He comes by, signs his credit card statement as if he's staying, but then he goes to the room, showers, and changes his clothes to something much more casual. His wife meets him in the parking lot. He leaves his car here and the two drive away. I don't know where, of course. He comes back Sunday night, spends the night, and leaves early Monday morning."

"He would pay for three nights, but stay one?" Paavo wanted to make sure he heard correctly.

"That's right. The maids started to talk about the guest who rarely slept in his bed. I was curious about it, and watched. They were right! As I said, on Sunday evening, he returns."

"Are you sure his wife was the person with him?" Paavo asked.

The clerk looked even more uncomfortable. "Um, maybe I shouldn't have said that, but the woman...she wasn't the type that looks like a girlfriend. She was kind of, I don't know...frumpy?"

"I see," Paavo said, even more confused. "Did you see the woman more than once?"

"I did. Every time."

Paavo nodded, then thanked the clerk as he handed him his card and explained that he was investigating Taylor

Bedford's murder.

As he left, he wondered who the woman was. He couldn't imagine anyone ever describing Mrs. Larina Bedford as frumpy.

Angie was in a house-hunting mood after her talk with Paavo the night before, but she wasn't one to settle on the first place she liked and could afford. When she learned Paavo would be out of town and probably not return to the city until quite late, she called Cat and informed her she wanted to spend the entire day—as long as it took—to check out every house that she could afford in the city, regardless of neighborhood, condition or anything else.

The hour was late when Angie stumbled back to her apartment and flopped down, exhausted, on the bed.

She had seen more houses than she thought possible, but refused to stop until she viewed them all. Caterina was ready to kill her before they reached the last one.

But now she knew. The house at 51 Clover Lane was more of a buy than she ever dreamed.

She wanted it.

Somehow, she would get it.

Chapter 8

GAIA WYNDOM HAD left a message on her bosses' phone early Monday morning saying she was ill and would need to take sick leave. Her boss thought it odd when she didn't show up or call on Tuesday, Wednesday, or Thursday, but hesitated to do anything because she was such a private person. Strangely private, in fact. He knew she lived alone and had no family. Finally he got up the nerve to phone her house on Thursday to see how she felt.

No one answer his call. The only emergency contact number in her personnel file listed a neighbor who sounded completely shocked that Ms. Wyndom would have given anyone her number as a 'contact.' The two never said more than "Hello" to each other.

The neighbor did say, however, that she had noticed Gaia's living room lights remained on all night for the past few days, which wasn't like Gaia at all. She normally shut off all lights by ten p.m. at the latest.

The supervisor thought and thought about it, and finally called the police. They sent someone who knocked on the door, but received no answer. On Friday, when she still hadn't shown up or answered any phone calls, the police entered her small, Sunset district home to investigate. And then called Homicide.

Officer Murphy, who secured the scene, let Paavo and Yosh into the apartment. The first thing he pointed out was a piece of notepaper in plain sight on the coffee table. They read it.

> *To Nobody:*
> *You, nobody, cared about me.*
> *You, nobody, loved me.*
> *When I needed you, nobody was there;*
> *When I cried alone at night, nobody comforted me.*
> *I cannot go on sharing my life with nobody.*
> *And so, I have decided to become nobody, too.*
>
> *Gaia, no more*

Officer Murphy then showed them the way to the bathroom. Gaia Wyndom, wearing a plain white nightgown, lay in a tub filled with water. No visible signs of how she had died were evident. Judging from the condition of the body, she had not been dead long.

It certainly looked like suicide, but homicide detectives were taught to never leap to conclusions. Clever murderers could fake a suicide and a suicide note. On the other hand, sometimes people did kill themselves.

Findings from the crime scene investigators and the forensics unit would tell quite a bit.

As Paavo and Yosh looked over the house to learn about the victim, the M.E. and her team arrived.

Gaia Wyndom was 43 years old, and had owned her house for twenty-two years. Paavo and Yosh could not find a single photo of her or anyone else in it. Both detectives looked through drawers and closets to find any bit of information about her. They found bank statements, utility bills and such, but nothing else—no diaries, journals, or anything similarly personal.

Even her medicine cabinet didn't have a single prescription in it. They started to wonder if she ever really lived in that house, but food filled the refrigerator as well as the pantry, clean dishes were ready to be put away in the dishwasher, and a few pieces of clothing were in a laundry basket.

"I can't remember seeing a house so empty of personality," Paavo said to Yosh as he went through drawers in Gaia's bedroom. "Nothing here indicates she had any contact with anyone else. Her mail was all bills, and her laptop had no e-mail except a couple pieces of spam. She may have wiped it clean. I'll get CSI to look into it."

Yosh checked her phone and saw it had no caller I.D., not even a last number redial feature. He then went out to the garage to look for boxes of memorabilia—old school yearbooks, anything at all to show Gaia Wyndom had a life. He came up empty.

"Does this make sense?" Paavo asked as the two stood in the living room of the eerily sterile house. The heat was on, but it felt cold.

Paavo walked back towards the bathroom where Officer Murphy stood watching the medical team working. He asked, "Who called in the death?"

"We got a report of a no-show from her place of employment. After twenty-four hours, we entered the house, found her, and called it in."

"It's amazing they noticed she was gone," Yosh said. "There's nothing here to indicate what kind of a person she was, what she liked, who she knew. Nothing."

"When did the employer last hear from her?" Paavo asked.

"Monday."

Paavo was surprised by that. "Five days ago. The body doesn't look as if she's been dead five days. If she killed herself, she must have thought about it for a few days before acting." He turned to the M.E. "Any thoughts on time of death, Evelyn?"

"I'm going to have to get back to the lab," Ramirez said. "The findings aren't making much sense, but the bath water could be complicating it. From the condition of the body, I guess—and it's only a guess—she's been dead a day or two."

"I wonder what she did all week," Paavo said.

"Maybe contemplating suicide, she threw away everything personal," Ramirez suggested, then returned to her team.

"I'll be most curious as to what people at her work say about her," Paavo said.

"Let's hope they don't find her as much a nobody as she felt herself to be," Yosh said with a nod to the suicide note on the coffee table.

Paavo faced to Murphy. "Do you have the name and phone number of the person who called in the missing person report, and her place of business?"

"I do." Murphy flipped through his papers. "A supervisor, Julio Sanchez, called us. The name of the company where she worked is Zygog Software in South City."

Paavo could scarcely believe what heard.

Yosh's mumbled comment was more to the point. "Holy shit!"

oOo

Paavo and Yosh returned to Zygog in South San Francisco. Now that two of its employees had been found dead, they spoke to the Chief Executive Officer to explain that their investigation at the company would be more wide-spread than it had been so far.

Yosh talked to Gaia Wyndom's supervisor and co-workers. She had chosen to work ten hours a day Monday through Thursday, with Fridays off. No one knew her well, and everyone said she seemed perpetually sad and perpetually tired. She only perked up when Taylor Bedford walked by, although no one had ever seen them say anything more than "hello" to each other. And now both were gone.

One person remarked on the fact that she had cut and styled her hair about six months ago, and that the new style looked much more attractive on her. She hoped that meant Gaia would come out of her shell, but she didn't. She never wore make-up, and her clothes were uniformly drab and matronly.

Paavo went to Taylor Bedford's office, where he found the secretary, Otto Link. Link appeared to be in his mid-forties or fifties, with short Grecian-formula brown hair to match his brown eyes, and a slight build. Paavo had spoken to him once before, but the man was so broken up over Bedford's death, he was scarcely coherent.

Link showed Paavo to Bedford's office. There, Paavo hunted through paperwork, datebooks, and e-mails to try to find any kind of connection with Gaia Wyndom.

He also did a more in depth review of Bedford's schedule, going back more than a year. He discovered that in the past six months Bedford's schedule had become much more stable than previously—two weeks out of town, and then two weeks in the office. Prior to that time, he varied his schedule, although about fifty percent of his working hours were spent on the road.

"Why did Mr. Bedford change from a week or a few days away here and there, to this very strict schedule of two weeks here and two away?" Paavo asked Link.

"He said he liked having a more set schedule," Link replied. "That way he'd always know if he would be in town or not."

"His wife said he worked weekends when away, wining and dining his clients."

"Oh?" Link smirked. "I'm sure I wouldn't know about that."

Link gave Paavo the addresses of every place Bedford visited over the six months prior to his death, as well as every hotel he stayed in. He saw that Bedford only charged the company for stays in Healdsburg every fourth weekend.

"Do you have any idea why Bedford would have been in the vicinity of Commercial and Kearney streets on Saturday night?" Paavo asked.

"None at all. It's close to the office, but we're closed on weekends."

"Any clients near there? Any favorite restaurants or bars he might have mentioned?"

"I can't say for sure." Otto looked perplexed. "He went to a lot of places around here. He liked a drink or two or ten, as is typical among salesmen as I'm sure you know."

"Do you know if Bedford knew Gaia Wyndom?" Paavo asked.

"I believe he did." Otto's mouth scrunched up as if he'd bitten into a lemon.

"Did they work together on projects or anything else?"

"She worked in the Records division where mail, e-mail, and telephone orders were maintained. She wasn't a manager, but a 'technical advisor' to the clerks who filed the company's paperwork. Mr. Bedford would only have reason to talk to her if had a problem, such as his clients not getting something on time or mistakes in billing. Salesmen almost never needed to go to Records."

"I see," Paavo said. That didn't help much.

Otto swallowed a couple of times before he asked, "Rumor has it Gaia committed suicide. But that's hard to believe. Do you think the two deaths are connected? Could the killer be someone here at work? Everyone's talking about it. We're all scared."

"We don't know that Ms. Wyndom was murdered," Paavo said. "Why is her suicide hard to believe?"

"She was very quiet. Hardly spoke to anyone, just did her work. When she did talk, her conversation was all about her cats, how being a vegetarian was morally superior, and the TV shows she watched. I mean, with her life, what would make her want to commit suicide? Nothing, I'd say."

"There were no cats in her house," Paavo said.

"Really?" Otto looked perplexed. "Maybe they died. Maybe that's why she killed herself! She was devoted to them."

"If you think of anything at all about either of them, give me a call." Paavo handed Otto his card.

Otto cocked his head then raised his eyebrows, and in a low voice asked, "How about over cocktails some evening?"

Paavo's eyes narrowed. "Did you and Mr. Bedford go out for cocktails?"

Otto gave a knowing grin. "We certainly did."

Paavo nodded. "Interesting. If you have something to discuss, you can find me at Homicide. Just call that number." He headed toward and elevator and hit the up button.

"Oh, all right. You can't get blame a guy for trying. These days, who knows?" Otto followed him, standing close as Paavo waited for the elevators. "The executive suites, I suppose."

"That's right," Paavo said.

"You've met Greenburg then?" Otto referred to the company's founder, Thomas Greenburg.

"He wasn't in last time I was here."

Link shrugged. "Wouldn't have mattered. If you expect to find out anything from Mr. Greenburg, you're going to be a very, very disappointed boy. Do come back and see me anytime."

The elevator doors opened, and Paavo got on. Alone.

Thirty-five year old Thomas Greenburg was a computer genius who started Zygog Software seven years earlier. It was now worth hundreds of millions of dollars and remained privately owned. Considering the problems Facebook and a few other software companies had when they tried to go public, Greenburg planned to keep it that way. There were other differences between Zygog and better known software businesses. One, it wasn't in Silicon Valley, and two, it made a huge profit based on a physical product, not simply advertising dollars.

A secretary directed Paavo down a long hall. She told him to knock on the door, and then as if to acknowledge that she knew that wasn't the way things were supposed to be done, she tightened her lips and gave a small shrug of the shoulders before spinning on her heel and returning to her desk.

Paavo knocked twice more before he heard a mumbled, "Come in."

Greenburg didn't stand or otherwise acknowledge him, but kept staring at his computer screen and occasionally hitting one key, then staring some more. He sat on the edge of his chair, elbows on his knees as he bent forward, eyeglasses just a few inches from the monitor. He wore a sweatshirt, Levis, and Nikes. The shoes seemed to be the most expensive thing in his office. His shaggy red hair looked uncombed and he looked unwashed.

Paavo waited a moment then moved closer, badge in hand. "Paavo Smith, Homicide. I'm here to talk to you about Taylor Bedford and Gaia Wyndom."

Greenburg hit another button, then pushed his glasses up on his nose and frowned. "I heard they were killed."

"Both are dead, yes," Paavo said.

"Terrible." Greenburg hit about ten keys in rapid succession.

"What do you know about them personally? Were they involved in anything new or unique here at work?"

At Greenburg's blank look, Paavo added, "Can you tell me anything about them?"

"Tell you?" Greenburg looked confused. "You can check with Personnel. Their evaluations are on record. Actually, everything's online. I can look them up for you." He immediately began pressing keys, paying no attention to Paavo who now stood right in front of him.

"No need," Paavo said. "They weren't killed because of their job performance. Were the two of them involved in anything together that you can think of? Any special programs, new products—anything at all tying them together?"

"No. I handle all new projects. They were Sales and Records, not the sort who work on R&D."

"How did they get along with their supervisors? With

other employees?"

Greenburg's eyes darted from one side to the other, then back to his computer monitor. "I don't know. I never heard of any problem with them."

Paavo stared at Greenburg a moment, then took a photo of Gaia from his folder. "Do you know this woman?"

Greenburg took the photo and stared at it. "I don't think so."

"What about him?" He handed Greenburg a photo of Bedford.

"Sure. He works here. I've seen him around a few times. Oh, wait...that's Bedford, isn't it? And the woman...is she the one killed? What was her name again?" He looked up at Paavo and didn't even seem embarrassed.

"Thank you, Mr. Greenburg." Paavo put the photos back in his folder. "I'll be in touch."

As he left the office, he could only think that Otto was right.

Chapter 9

Angie was thrilled when Paavo called to invite her to a quick dinner. He had managed to take a look at the record of the Sea Cliff murders and wanted to fill her in before he went back to Homicide. He knew he faced a long night there.

They met at an Indian restaurant. Over chicken vindaloo, shrimp masala, vegetable samosas, and naan, he told her all he had learned. Angie took in every word.

Eric and Natalie Fleming had been married for only eight months and lived at 51 Clover Lane when they were found shot to death near the edge of the cliff overlooking China Beach.

The way the bodies were situated, it appeared Natalie had been running away from Eric when he shot and killed her. Supposedly, he then turned the gun on himself with a bullet to the temple.

They had been dead two days before their bodies were discovered. No one had reported hearing the gunshots because no one in that neighborhood believed that was what they heard—most assumed they had heard a car backfiring.

A trace of gunpowder residue had been found on Eric's

clothes, but it wasn't enough to decide he had fired the gun, just that the gun had been near him when fired. They found no gunpowder on his hands, but a light rain had fallen and could have washed it away.

Everyone who knew them said they were a devoted couple with no hint of a rocky marriage. Natalie was beautiful, glamorous, and an heiress. Eric had made money moving from one Silicon Valley start-up to another, just as many young computer nerds did back in those halcyon days, and he stopped working altogether after his marriage to enjoy life with his rich wife. Eric was described as a lover, not a fighter. No one could believe he even owned a gun, let alone would use it on his wife. Also, no one believed anyone would want to kill them.

The gun found at the scene, the murder weapon, was unregistered. The investigating detectives, now both retired, had refused to state that Eric Fleming had murdered his wife. Instead, they put everything in the cold case files, meaning the murder remained unresolved to this day.

Angie shook her head. "Two young people, in love, newly married, no money worries, no employment issues, no known problems...and then they were dead. How horrible! I wonder what really happened to them."

"I can't tell you. The investigators could find no motive."

"There's got to be a reason. Even if it was a random shooting, there's got to be some sign—other similar deaths, a madman in the area, something."

"Their car's disappearance adds to the mystery," Paavo said. "Eric owned a two-seater Mercedes sports car. It didn't turn up until a year later, half-in and half-out of the Russian River. Some kids were hiking in a rugged part of

Sonoma County and found it. Other than that, no one found anything to explain what had happened to the couple."

Angie pursed her lips. "Maybe the investigators simply weren't looking in the right places."

"There's not much more to be done. Maybe they didn't perform the most complete investigation, but it happened thirty years ago." Just then his cell phone rang, and he took the call. He wasn't on it long. "More forensics results are in. I've got to get going."

She nodded. "Okay. I appreciate the information you found."

He put money on the table for the bill and tip, then helped her with her coat. "Now that you know what happened, you're going to decide about the house on its own merits, right?"

She didn't look happy, but she agreed. "I can do that."

"How is it you have a key to this place?" Stan asked Angie as they stood on the front porch of the 51 Clover Lane house. "Don't you need to be a realtor to have one?"

After learning about the Flemings and their death, plus Paavo's opinion that a murder near the house wasn't a game changer as far as he was concerned, she wanted to see the house one more time. Since Paavo had to return to Homicide, she called Stan.

"My sister's a realtor," Angie said as she unlocked the front door.

"That doesn't answer my question," Stan pointed out.

"Some things you don't want to know," Angie said as she slipped the original house key back into the lock box, then put the copy she had made into her purse. It took her all of a minute to have the front door key duplicated at a hardware store. If Angie told Cat what she had done, Cat would have thrown a fit. But that was just for show. She was sure Cat left her with the key so she could copy it. After all, Cat knew she wouldn't steal anything from the house, and also knew she would want to visit it about three dozen times before making up her mind about the place. The last thing Cat wanted was to drive back and forth from Tiburon to escort her on all those visits.

"Anyway, Cat talked to the owner, and she's so happy that someone is serious about possibly buying the house, she told Cat I should feel free to come and go as often as I like. She's even willing to give me a lease-option if I wish. Here we go." Angie swung open the door and let Stan enter.

"This place has style, doesn't it?" he said as he wandered through the large living and dining room, inspecting the woodwork and hardwood floors. "An older home that has been beautifully remodeled to take advantage of the setting."

Angie put the candy dish she'd bought to replace the broken one on the coffee table, then followed him as he strolled into the kitchen. "You'll have to gut this," he said with a frown.

"Not immediately. If I change out the old appliances, the rest can wait."

He turned on a burner on the range. "At least it's gas, not electric. That helps."

Angie led him to the bedrooms, starting with the two upstairs, and ending with the master.

"Large. Nice view," he said, then walked into the master bath. "It should be much more plush."

Stan opened the sliding glass door in the master bedroom and stepped out to a private deck overlooking the ocean. "As much as I love my apartment, I miss being able to step outside and be surrounded by nature. This is quite nice, and in the back yard you have room to put in a little garden, maybe herbs, or even a few flowers. People always told me I have a green thumb."

"I didn't know that about you," Angie said.

"Yes. I used to grow a lot of houseplants. Talk to them and mist them daily, that's the trick." He leaned back against the banister surrounding the deck and looked at the house. "Pleasant house, this."

"That's what I told you."

"A good deal, you said?"

"An excellent deal."

"Well, if you don't want it, let me know," Stan said, his expression a portrait of sorrow. "My apartment won't be the same without you living across the hall. And if you're still there after you're married, it'll mean I've got that big cop watching my every step." He reached out and took her hand. "I know he's jealous of me because of our relationship, Angie. For that reason, I know I won't be comfortable staying there."

She could scarcely believe she heard right. Paavo, jealous of Stan? He was even more delusional than she imagined. She pulled her hand free and then patted his shoulder. "Stan, don't be ridiculous. If I leave, I'll make sure to tell my father to only rent to someone who's a good cook."

"You're mocking me now." He turned around to face the water and, bending at the waist, rested his forearms on the railing as he stared out at the ocean. "I can't imagine living there without you nearby. I'll have to move. If you don't take this house, I may have to buy it."

"Now you're being melodramatic!" Angie mimicked his

pose, enjoying the ocean view herself. "Did I tell you there's something strange about this place? That many people have attempted to buy it, but the deal always fell through?"

"You never mentioned that. What's the problem with it?"

"It might be..." Angie paused a beat, and then hit him with: "because there was a murder."

"A what?" His eyes widened and he stood up straight.

Angie relayed all she had learned from Paavo.

"That story gives me goose bumps. I think I've just changed my mind about wanting to live here," Stan said.

"Good, because I've decided I don't care," Angie announced. "I like this house, in fact, I love it! I mean, it's not as if their ghosts are haunting the place."

Just then, they heard a crash from the living room.

They gawked at each other, and then rushed inside. The vase that had been on the small round table now lay broken on the hardwood floor, its silk flowers spread around it. The vase was the one that seemed to re-center itself on the table the last time Angie visited.

"What happened?" Stan asked, his eyes bulging.

"Why don't you shut the bedroom's sliding glass door?" Angie said uneasily. "It must have caused some sort of a draft."

"A damned strong draft!" Stan muttered as he stepped into the bedroom to shut the door.

Angie picked up the pieces of the white porcelain vase and the silk flowers. "I guess I'll be looking for a replacement."

"That gave me a bit of a start." Stan chuckled. Back in the living room, he sat on the green and gold sofa, his hands clasped behind his head, elbows out, feet crossed on the coffee table as he studied the room, the view, the setting. "This house is definitely not right for you and Paavo. He works with murders. Living here would be too much like work for him. Besides, you'd have to completely redecorate it. Get rid of all the frou-frou, use sleeker lines in the furniture to open the place up. Add color to the walls. I think my interior decorator friend, Ernesto, would either laugh himself to death or die of shock if he saw this place."

The candy dish Angie had just replaced rose up off the coffee table. Stan watched it in horror. "What?"

He jumped to his feet. Angie froze. The two stared slack-jawed as the dish hovered, then moved back from Stan a moment before it rocketed towards him as if hurled from a sling-shot. Stan ducked just in time. The dish sailed past him and hit a wall.

Stan let out a high-pitched, blood-curdling scream, and ran behind Angie. A book slid out of the bookshelf and now it too floated in mid-air: Umberto Eco's *The Name of the Rose,* probably the biggest book on the shelf.

"Run!" Angie cried. But she needn't have bothered. Stan pushed her out of the way and was the first one out the door. Angie followed close behind.

Behind them, the door slammed shut, and then the deadbolt clicked into place.

Chapter 10

LATE THAT NIGHT when Paavo arrived home, he found Angie in his living room, asleep on the couch. His cat Hercules lay curled up asleep beside her, a half-eaten bowl of popcorn on the floor and the TV on. "What's this?" he asked, going to her. "Is something wrong?"

"No," she said groggily as she opened her eyes and sat up. "I just didn't want to be alone."

Despite her words that nothing was wrong, he knew her better than that. He sat and held her.

She said she had been stressing too much over the wedding and their living arrangements, and that she was "practically seeing things"—with emphasis on the word practically.

He had no idea what was really bothering her, but if he was patient, eventually she would explain. For the moment, simply having her turn to him when she needed comfort meant a lot to him.

The next morning, as Paavo headed out the door, he found it even more difficult to leave Angie sleeping in his bed, in his house, than in her apartment. He wondered if he would feel this way after they were married, as well. He did know one thing, though. Seeing her in his home made him feel better about himself than leaving her in her father's building. He supposed, in these modern time, such thinking was old-fashioned, backward, and macho, but nonetheless, he felt more like a man, a provider, with her there.

Maybe she was right when she said they should find a home of their own rather than live in her father's apartment.

When he arrived at work, he learned the autopsies had been completed.

Gaia Wyndom had ingested a large number of sleeping pills, enough to kill a woman of her size and weight. No other signs of struggle or trauma were found. The M.E. said it could have been suicide, but she couldn't be certain if Gaia purposefully took the pills, or someone drugged her. The state of the body, however, was confusing.

She had been found in a bath, so presumably the water would have been comfortably warm before she got in—not even suicides got into tubs of cold, uncomfortable water. Warm water should have sped up decomposition. The small amount of decomposition indicated she had been dead only a day or two, yet other bodily functions appeared to have ceased much earlier. The reports were confused. The M.E. said she needed more time to run tests and research exactly what had happened to the woman. The finding would make more sense if she had gotten into ice water, but that was hard to imagine.

If she had been alive all week, where had she been prior to her death? What had she been doing? The time of death inconsistencies made it difficult to determine what had happened to her.

Taylor Bedford's autopsy results were much clearer.

He had been killed by a knife at least seven inches long in the shape of a chef's carving knife. It entered under the ribcage and jabbed upward, piercing the heart. A second stab in the same area assured his quick death.

Whoever did it apparently took his wallet and cellphone. They weren't found in or near the dumpster or in the garbage truck.

The autopsies were interesting, but didn't tell Paavo much he didn't already know. No matter when Gaia died, she had been alive at the time of Taylor's murder. He knew that because Taylor's death happened Saturday night, and Gaia called in sick on Monday morning. People at work had indicated she had a crush on him. Did she try to act on it and he spurned her so she killed him and then herself out of remorse and guilt?

When he returned from discussing the autopsy results with the M.E., he decided to look more closely into Thomas Greenburg, founder of Zygog.

Greenburg bothered him. He seemed uninterested in anything about his two dead employees, while everyone else in the building worried that Zygog could be somehow involved, perhaps with a madman targeting its employees for some crazed reason.

Paavo quickly discovered a slew of online magazine articles and Internet sites about Greenburg. All talked about Greenburg as cold, nerdy, and aloof, a man who lived in his own world, unhampered and uninterested in anyone else. He started out as a game creator and quickly moved into online hacking. By the time he was twenty, he claimed the ability to hack into any database, anywhere. Ten years ago, at age twenty-five, an anonymous angel gave him $300,000 to put his skills to useful purposes and start a business.

He started slow with an innovative inventory system set up for people whose inventory all looked basically the same to the unskilled eye, but where the slightest error in calibration could mean the difference between success and disaster of a project.

In time, he expanded to other products and within three years, he established Zygog Software. Its profits doubled every year for the first five years, and now it hummed along at a fine clip.

The information was interesting, but it didn't bring Paavo any closer to figuring out who killed Gaia and Taylor.

Chapter 11

"YOU'VE TOLD ME many times that Nana Cirmelli knew all about ghosts and spirits and demons," Angie said as she sat in her mother's kitchen with a cup of coffee and some hard, round Italian cookies with white sugary icing on top. The cookies were Angie's favorite, but could only be eaten by dunking them into hot coffee to make them soft enough to avoid breaking a tooth.

"Not only that." Serefina Teresa Maria Giuseppina Amalfi, all 5'1", 150 pounds of her shuddered as she said, "She knew about the evil eye!"

Serefina put her forefinger below her eye and pulled down the lower lid—her family's signal for the evil eye, or *malocchio*. Angie learned on a recent trip to Italy that old ideas like the evil eye, brought to the US by Italian immigrants in the early 1900's and still talked about here, were pretty much laughed at in Italy. Not around Serefina, however, despite her refusal to say she believed in it.

Stories of old women who could give the evil eye had terrified Angie as a child. Simply receiving a compliment from a jealous person could cause the evil eye to descend on the one being complimented. Mothers had to be especially careful that their babies weren't cursed. If someone praised a cute baby's looks, the mother had to be sure to say, "God bless her (or him)" to ward off the attack.

When eight-year-old Angie heard that salt warded it off as well, she put thimble-size amounts of salt into plastic wrap and held them shut with rubber bands. She put the packets on doorframes and window frames in the bedroom she shared with her sister Frannie. One day, Serefina hired a painter, and more than a little fuss was caused when he found them. Serefina leapt to the idea that one of her older daughters was doing drugs. She yelled at Bianca, Caterina and Maria, threatening terrible things would happen to all of them if the culprit didn't confess. Finally, Angie piped up that it was salt, and she did it to protect the family.

Serefina tasted it. Angie told the truth.

Neither Angie nor Serefina ever talked about the evil eye again after that happened. Until now.

"Did Nana believe in ghosts?" Angie asked, knowing her mother, who tried to act modern and practical, would never admit to such a thing about herself.

"*Sì,* of course. Everyone believed such nonsense back in the old country."

"What did they say about them? Are they dangerous, harmful, scary, or like Caspar the Friendly Ghost?"

"You have to know why they're still in this world. Some good, some bad. But mostly bad." Serefina quickly added, "Or that's what I been told. I don't believe in such things."

"Of course not," Angie said.

"But many, many people I know have experienced the spirit of someone close to them visiting them soon after dying. Maybe to say goodbye, or to see them one last time." She took a deep breath then said, "It's hard to believe, but that may have happened to me once." Serefina turned her head and looked out the window at the sky as the memory filled her. "I'm not saying it did. And many times, I told myself it was just a coincidence, a dream, but sometimes, I wonder. Anyway, one night—you were very young—I was sleeping, and suddenly woke up. There, at the foot of my bed, stood my father. I hadn't seen him in many years because he lived in Italy, and with five children, your father and I didn't have the money to visit him very often."

"Go on, Mamma," Angie said when Serefina stopped talking.

"I swear to my dying day, on the Madonna herself, I was awake and saw him looking down at me. He smiled. '*Papà?*' I said, I was so surprised! '*Ti amo, gioia mia,*' he told me. It was his voice, I'm sure of it. He looked at peace, and then he said for me not to be sad.

"At that, your father woke up and asked why I was sitting up talking to myself. What could I say? I saw that I was all alone now. So, I said I had a dream, and told him to go back to sleep. Not an hour later, early in the morning, I received a call from Nana. She told me that my papà had died about three hours earlier. I knew, then, he had come to see me one last time. That he loved me so much...it still warms my heart."

Angie clasped her mother's hand. "Of course he did, Mamma. You've told me so many stories about him. He loved you very much."

Serefina sighed deeply as she dunked another cookie in her coffee, then took a big bite before going on. Cookies helped the sadness go away. "Anyway, that's not what most people think when they talk about ghosts. They think of miserable souls, stuck on this earth because something bothers them or is unfinished and they can't rest."

"Stuck here," Angie murmured. For some reason, the idea resonated within her. Not that she believed in ghosts.

She and Stan, as they sat quivering with coffee and brandy in her apartment after their scare at Clover Lane, convinced themselves that bright sunlight had bounced off the candy dish in a way that made them think it moved, that their running had caused the book shelves to shake and topple a book, and that they had simply managed to scare themselves with their jokes. Of course there were no such things as ghosts!

"That makes sense," she said after a while.

"What makes sense?"

"Nothing." Angie gulped down the rest of her coffee and stood up.

Determination filled her. If she was tempted to believe in ghosts, this house nonsense had gone too far. Time to cease and desist! She needed to forget all about the house in the Sea Cliff and its self-propelled books and candy dishes.

She didn't care how cheap, beautiful, or anything else it was. And she especially didn't care what kind of creatures did or did not live in it, or if they had issues that caused them to be 'stuck' on this earth. None of it meant anything to her any longer. She had a wedding to plan. "Thank you, Mamma. You've been a big help."

"*Aspetti!* Wait!" Serefina stood and followed Angie to the door. "I don't know why you're asking about such things, and I'm not saying I believe in them, but remember, Angelina, the words of Sant'Agostino. He said that evil always tries to disguise itself as good. There is evil in this world. You've seen it, I know, and if you get involved with dark forces, it is not easy to tell which are good and which are bad. It is best to keep away from them, all of them. Be careful, Angelina. And be wary."

Angie nodded. Her mother's words only confirmed her

decision. "Don't worry. Everything will be fine now."

Connie was stunned to see Stan Bonnette walk into her gift shop. "What a surprise. Are you looking for a present for someone?"

"I'm worried," he said, taking a chocolate mint patty from the tray by the cash register. "It's about Angie's fixation with the house that's for sale in the Sea Cliff. I need you to tell me everything is really fine."

"Everything is really fine," Connie said. "Now, what's this about?"

"Ghosts." He unwrapped the patty. "I'm sure she thinks she's seeing them."

"Nonsense!"

"It's true! She's obsessed with them. She should be thinking about other things, such as, does she really want to marry a cop? Personally, I have my doubts, but that's just me. Anyway, I think she's got so many pressures with her upcoming wedding and her lack of a good job, and now worrying about where she and Paavo will live, that instead of dealing with everything, she's seeing spirits!" He bit into the chocolate. "Mmm!"

"She hasn't said anything like that to me," Connie insisted. "Frankly, I think you're the one who's delusional! And that'll be fifty cents."

"I was with her at the house. A gust of wind came through because we had the doors open, and you'd think she saw Banquo's ghost from Macbeth. It was ludicrous. She actually ran screaming out of there."

"She ran screaming?" Connie asked.

"Yes! It's true," Stan confided. He tossed the wrapper into the wastebasket, but didn't reach for his wallet.

"What did you do?"

"I ran out after her. What else could I do? I had to make sure she was all right. I think she's losing it."

"Maybe we should talk to Paavo," Connie said.

"Hell, no! I'm the last person he'd listen to." He reached for another mint and she slapped his hand. "Ouch! Anyway, he knows how Angie feels about me, and I think he resents our relationship. Leave him out of it."

Connie knew the real reason Stan didn't want to talk to Paavo. Stan was intimidated by him and turned into a babbling bowl of gelatinous goo whenever Paavo was near. "All right," Connie said. "If we don't talk to Paavo, what can we do?"

"That's obvious," Stan said. "We need to convince Angie that she doesn't want to live in that house. She's perfectly safe and happy in her apartment. She should stay there." He didn't say, but mentally added *"Alone."*

He then took a dollar out of his pocket and put it on the counter.

"Thank you," she said. "But that's the price for two. I'll get you change."

"No need." He picked up two more patties and walked out of the shop.

While Paavo continued to track down anyone who could give him information about the shadowy Gaia Wyndom, Yosh pursued leads on Taylor Bedford. He gained no information other than "Taylor wasn't himself lately," from friends, family and co-workers until he found a bar three blocks from the crime scene.

"Sure I remember Taylor Bedford," Donny Petrollini, the bartender at Harrigan's said. "He had to go on the road all the time for his job, but when he was in town, he stopped in every night after work. He would drink and get pretty well lit, then call a cab. I think he didn't want to face his wife."

When drinking, Taylor would tell Donny about his miserable life. "He spent two weeks in town at a time—two work weeks. He told me he hated his home life so much, he'd leave the city on a Friday night for his business trip, and not return until Sunday, two weeks later. Finally, I asked him, 'Taylor,' I says, 'I never heard of no one leaving home early and coming home late from a business trip.' Well, he had drunk enough that he says, 'Who says I'm spending my weekends working?'" Donny chuckled.

"Did he ever explain?" Yosh asked.

"He didn't have to. He had a woman on the side. Sounded like love, if you ask me. I mean, he'd spend three weekends with her. I'm surprised his wife didn't kill him. Hey, maybe she did."

Donny went on to say that the last couple of months, Taylor wasn't as happy as usual. He told the bartender that he had decided to leave his wife. He was crazy about 'my girl,' as he called her, and he couldn't stand that when they were at work, she pretended there was nothing between them.

"Wait...he said he worked with the other woman?" Yosh asked.

"That's right." Donny explained that Taylor told him the company had a very strict no-fraternization policy, and his girl insisted that they act like complete strangers at work. They could both be fired—or more likely, she would be. Taylor kept telling her he wanted to marry her, but she kept saying no. He wanted to tell his wife, tell his company, tell the whole world, that he loved her.

Taylor said his wife looked like every man's dream, but beauty was all she had. He claimed the only thing she ever loved was her mirror. He didn't even know why she married him.

His girl, on the other hand, was fun, fascinating, had a wild imagination, and did everything with great enthusiasm, including making love. Taylor said he had never been around anyone with such a lust for life. That was why, at work, he couldn't handle the drab way she dressed and acted.

Donny thought a moment. "I'm remembering one time something weird happened. He was real shook up the day it took place—just a day or two before he left on his last business trip. He cornered her in the supply room and kissed her. She burst into tears and ran off. He said it felt like kissing a stranger. It shook him, and he didn't know what had happened to her. He couldn't take it anymore. He said he didn't like her looking so dowdy either. He knew the real woman. He said he wanted to stop living a lie. I never saw him after that, and now I learn he's dead. Poor guy; I guess he got his wish."

Yosh nodded.

Donny leaned on the bar and looked at Yosh. "You know what was really sad about the guy? I think I was the only one he ever really opened up to about all this. He gave me the impression that his whole life, except for me and his weekends with his girl, was make-believe. He was a good guy, and a good tipper. I'm gonna miss the poor schlub."

Chapter 12

A NGIE DECIDED TO GO to the next prospective wedding planner's place of business after the irritating experience of Diane LaGrande seizing on a wedding theme based on her Cezanne lithograph. Now, Angie found herself in the back of a wedding gown shop. She glanced at the dresses as she entered, but she didn't find one that jumped out at her as "the" dress.

Nancy Blum, wedding planner, was a tall, thin woman, pretty enough to have been a fashion model. She greeted Angie and had her sit on the opposite side of her desk.

"Here are some pictures of weddings I've done in the past," she said, handing Angie a thick photo album. While Angie turned the pages, Nancy asked questions about the type of wedding she hoped for, the size, location, and so on.

The weddings in the photos were lovely but, to Angie's eye, nothing special. There wasn't one unique thing about them from the cakes, to the flower arrangements, to the reception halls, to the combos for live music. The brides' dresses and veils were unexceptional, and the same for the bridesmaids' dresses.

Boring.

"So, let's talk in specifics about the wedding you hope

for," Nancy said.

"Something traditional, yet unique," Angie said, handing back the album.

"Yes, that's what everyone says," Nancy said dismissive sigh. "We can do that. We *always* do that. Rose bouquets, matchbooks and candles as favors. I've got it covered. But tell me, what are your interests? Do you work? What about the groom? What does he do?"

"My main interest is in cooking. I've had a variety of jobs involved with haute cuisine, but nothing currently. My fiancé is a homicide inspector."

"Oh. Well...let's see. We could have a huge variety of foods at the wedding dinner."

"Yes, we could," Angie said, not impressed. "I'll take care of the food."

Nancy's face suddenly brightened. "Did you say the groom is a homicide detective?"

"Yes, we call them inspectors in San Francisco."

"You know, you might be one of the few people who actually can have a unique wedding! Few can, you know. Most brides and grooms have incredibly boring jobs in big office buildings or shops. But for you, oh my God! We can actually do something fun"

She suddenly jumped to her feet. Angie just gawked at her. "Finally, something different from the usual! I know, let's get crazy!"

"Crazy?" Angie gulped.

"We can put yellow crime scene tape all around the reception hall! And maybe draw a chalk figure on the floor, you know, where the body was found. In fact, we could draw two chalk figures, a bride and a groom! Wouldn't that be hilarious!"

"Hilarious?" Angie said, horrified at the idea.

Nancy didn't notice. "Of course! The wedding as the scene of the crime! That is truly unique! And you said you'll be getting married in a church, right?"

Angie blanched, having a good guess as to what was coming. "Correct. A very old world, traditional Catholic church."

"Hmm...I wonder if they'd let us put crime scene tape up and down the aisle. They shouldn't object to that. Oh! Oh! Another idea! We could use toy guns—squirt guns—as party favors! Your guests could have so much fun shooting each other! And you and the groom! I'm just loving it! I've done so many weddings that are all alike. Every last one of them, the same thing over and over and over. But this, I'm loving! And I can tell you're loving it, too, aren't you?"

Without saying a word, Angie stood up and left the shop.

Angie wasn't surprised when Paavo came to her apartment that night. She knew she had worried him the night before, showing up at his place because she'd been so frightened by the strangeness on Clover Street. She had worried herself, and had replayed in her head every horror film she had ever seen until fatigue overtook her.

Now, she wanted to tell him that episode in her life was over. She had already forgotten about the house...mostly. But first, she put her arms around him and kissed him. "I'm glad you're here," she said, enjoying staring into his translucent blue eyes.

"So am I." He continued to hold her. "I've now got two murders instead of one and I expect things to heat up soon. But tonight, I'm free and I'd like to see the house you're so excited about. I've been thinking about what you said about us finding our own place." He drew her closer, studying her as he added, "You're right. We need to do that."

She stepped back and gaped at him. "I am?"

"Definitely." He smiled. "I like the idea. A lot."

"Uhhh..."

His brows crossed slightly. "Have you changed your mind about it?"

"No." Even to her ear, her voice sounded strangely high.

"Good! The Sea Cliff house sounds like a real find. And if the murders of tenants thirty years ago have other buyers spooked, we might be able to get it at an even better price."

Angie shivered at the word "spooked." Paavo didn't notice.

"That could be." She scooted over to the coffee table and started straightening the bridal magazines spread over it.

"Have you changed your mind?" he asked.

"No."

He stared at her, then sat on the sofa. "What's going on, Angie?" When she didn't answer right away, he continued. "Is this about the murders? You've been through enough cases with me to know there's nothing to be afraid of. Murders are rare, but they happen in big cities. You've never let that kind of thing bother you before."

She put down the magazines, took a few deep breaths and said, "You're right." She nodded. "It shouldn't bother me."

"Good. So...shall we go see it?"

Her mind roiled. If she told him her earlier decision, she would sound like an idiot.

"Angie?" he said.

She walked over to the picture window, looking out at

the lights of the city rather than facing him. "Well..."

He watched her, then stepped up behind her and wrapped his arms around her shoulders. Drawing her back against him, he kissed her ear, her cheek, then said. "Tell me what's the matter. Did someone else beat us to it?"

"No...that's not it."

"Are we unable to see it for some reason?"

"No...Caterina, uh, gave me a key. She knows how interested I was. Am."

"Well, then?"

She turned to face him. She felt as if the word stuck in her throat, but finally she forced it out, and squawked, "Okay."

Angie unlocked the door and slowly, nervously, pushed it open. She stuck her head inside. "Hello!" she called loudly. "We're here to see the house. Is anybody home? It's Angelina Amalfi and Inspector Paavo Smith of the San Francisco Police Department!"

"Angie, what are you doing?" Paavo asked. "The whole neighborhood doesn't need to know our names. Besides, I thought you said the house is empty."

"It is, but sometimes other people come to see it, and if anyone else is here"—she swallowed hard—"I want to be sure they know you're a cop and we shouldn't be messed with."

"This is hardly an area where you have to worry about such things," Paavo said. "Are you going to let us in, or will we spend the night on the front porch?"

"You're right, since we're here, you should see it. It's just that it's not daytime. In the daylight you'd be able to see how beautiful the view is, and in the dark, you can't and—"

He reached around her, pushed the door open and walked in. He flipped on the lights, and Angie could see his amazement. He didn't say a word as went through the living, dining and kitchen areas, then returned to the living room, opened the sliding glass door to the garden and stepped out.

The moon sat low on the horizon, casting a ray of light onto the ocean. The area around them was so dark they could see thousands of stars overhead, a rare occurrence in foggy San Francisco where even on clear nights the city lights were so bright few stars were visible. The waves lapping on the beach far below created a serene, calming sound. Even Angie, despite her angst at what would greet them inside the house, had to admit that the heavens were putting on quite a show for Paavo.

When he finally spoke, his voice sounded soft and awe-filled. "It's not daylight, but even now, I can get a sense of how beautiful this is."

"It is, isn't it?" she said. His expression was serious, thoughtful. "Do you think, Paavo, we could be happy here?"

He faced her. "To be wherever you are, Angel, makes me happy. I don't want or need anything else."

"That's how I feel, too," she said and kissed him.

They went back inside and he saw that the master bedroom had the same ocean view as the main rooms. "Hmm...someone wearing perfume must have been in here recently," Paavo said. "It's a good scent. I like it."

Angie noticed it, too—just as she'd noticed it earlier with Caterina. But now, realizing it wasn't Cat's perfume, she recognized the scent. Her mother used all the time when Angie was young—Joy by Jean Patou. Her heart started to pound. Who would have been here wearing it?

Paavo quickly took in the master bedroom and bath, the room Angie called a "den or nursery," and the two bedrooms and bath upstairs.

Angie tried to ignore the perfume, which seemed to follow them wherever they went. But she couldn't, and grew more nervous with each passing moment.

"Let's see the garage," Paavo said.

Angie led him to it. "There's a big area in the back with room for tools, a lawn mower, all kinds of stuff."

"I'll have to buy a lawn mower if we live here." Paavo slung his arm over Angie's shoulders. "I guess that'll mean I'm really a married man."

His simple words touched her heart. "A rite of passage, I'd say. But no matter where we live, you'll really be a married man." She smiled up at him. "I know seeing this at night isn't ideal. You can't tell a thing about the paint, the roof, the yard...all those important things. But as to the feel of the place, the layout...?"

They returned to the living room and she watched him look over the woodwork, the large stone fireplace, the hardwood floors, high ceilings. "It's a good house for us," he said. "You're right that I'd want to see it in daylight, but I find it hard to imagine that my impression will change."

Paavo's positive reaction thrilled her. The house put on quite a show for him, she thought. For the first time, she felt welcome here...despite the perfume. What had she been worried about?

She watched him as he stood at the living room windows and looked out at the ocean, the big tough detective who was also the kindest, most gentle man she had ever known. Yes, she thought. She could see the two of them happily living in this house.

"What are you thinking, Paavo?" she asked stepping to

his side.

His hand clasped hers. "I know you've got some concerns about this house's past."

"Not me!" she said quickly. "It was all Connie's fault! She pointed out that with the furniture here, she felt as if the prior tenants could walk into the house at any time—that she felt their presence! But Cat explained the furniture is simply to 'stage' the house so it looks better."

"Connie, hum?" he said.

"That's right!" she insisted.

"So if we bought the house, the furniture stays?"

"No way! For one thing, all this furniture is over thirty years old!"

"Practically antiques," Paavo said, trying not to smile.

"I particularly can't wait to get rid of that sofa." She pointed to the overly modern, low back, no arm sofa in moss green with gold lame stripes. "It's butt-ugly, if you ask me."

Just then, a watercolor of a mountain lake in the dining area fell off the wall. Angie started so badly she nearly jumped out of her skin.

Paavo went over to it and found that the nail still protruded from the wall, so he simply had to lift the picture up and rehang it. "Odd," he said.

That did it! Wide-eyed, she looked all around. Time to get out. No sense pushing her luck. "Let's lock up and get out of here," she said, speaking more rapidly than she thought possible. "I'm suddenly ravenous for dinner. Let's find a place to eat. Fast!"

Chapter 13

GAIA WYNDOM'S CELL phone bill lay on Paavo's desk when he arrived at Homicide the next morning. He had been unable to find any indication that she had a cell phone in her home, and even her employment records showed only a landline. The landline showed no personal calls beyond her boss trying to check on her health. Once again, Paavo had been left wondering if the woman had any kind of a life.

Yet, indications were that she had an affair with Taylor Bedford, hard though it was to believe. She might have had a split personality but they still needed some way to communicate.

He did a check of AT&T, Sprint, Verizon, and T-Mobile—the big carriers in the San Francisco area—and sure enough, a cell phone record for her showed up with AT&T.

Call after call went to one number only—Taylor Bedford's cell phone. Long calls were made in the evening, and just a few short ones on weekends. The pattern of calls confirmed the story the bartender at Harrigan's told Yosh. Taylor Bedford and Gaia Wyndom were having an affair.

He looked over Bedford's cell service and discovered

he had two cell phones, along with a family landline. One was for calls related to his business and his wife; the second was exclusively for Gaia.

From what he and Yosh had learned about the two victims, it was hard to imagine them together. But then Otto Link had also made suggestive comments about Bedford. Maybe he was the Casanova of the tool and die trade.

Paavo called Larina Bedford into Homicide. She had acted so poised and self-assured at her home, he wanted her in a less comfortable environment.

Homicide's administrative assistant escorted her to the interview room. Paavo allowed her to sit alone in it for nearly ten minutes before joining her. The windowless room, with cameras in the ceiling, one gray metal table and four cold, hard metal chairs was intimidating. It often made people so nervous they couldn't hide their lies.

While Yosh observed from outside the room, Paavo entered it.

"Do you have news, Inspector?" Larina said without even a preliminary "hello." She appeared to be anything but intimidated.

"Something new has turned up." He sat across from her and opened a folder, taking out Gaia Wyndom's photo. "Do you know this woman?"

Larina looked at it a long moment. "I do not."

"She also worked at Zygog, and also died suspiciously just days after your husband. Does that help your memory any?"

"There's no reason why it should," Larina looked him steadily in the eye. "I did read in the newspaper about a death at Zygog, but that was a suicide, as I recall."

"Her name was Gaia Wyndom. She made a number of

phone calls to your husband."

Larina folded her hands, resting them on the table. "They apparently worked together. Taylor spent weeks at a time out of the office. How else was she supposed to reach him? Carrier pigeon?"

"The calls were off hours, to a cell phone different from the one he used for everyone else. You, included."

"My husband worked twenty-four-seven, Inspector. He had no 'off hours.' If he called and wanted something, he would expect a reply anytime of the day or night. If they had a special way to contact each other, I'm sure they had a business reason for it."

"I spoke with many of Mr. Bedford's customers, and they said he never took them out to dinner or anywhere else."

Larina's face flushed red. "They're lying. They don't want anyone to know what he gave them! If they admitted to receiving gifts, they're afraid the IRS will tax them. Instead, they deny, deny, deny."

"The clerk at your husband's favorite motel in Healdsburg said Mr. Bedford would check into the motel, but rarely sleep there."

She grimaced. "A motel clerk gives you your information? For all you know, Taylor didn't tip him or the housekeepers and they decided to make trouble. I don't know or care. Now, it appears to me you've wasted my time by asking about some dead person at Zygog. Was she killed in the same manner as my husband?"

"No, she wasn't."

"Do you have any proof that my husband cheated on me?" she asked stiffly.

"Do you?"

She stood. "This interview is over, Inspector. If you

want to speak to me again, call my lawyer."

He showed her to the door.

"If" ghosts were real, Angie told herself, and if someone were murdered and the police gave up looking for his or her killer, that dead person could be plenty angry, perhaps angry enough to stick around this mortal coil in a non-corporeal form.

But ghosts weren't real.

The only real people in this scenario were the two who were dead, and whoever killed them.

Suddenly Angie realized what had been troubling her. It had nothing to do with ghosts at all, but with her far too active imagination. People told her she fantasized too much.

Now, she made up wild stories and came up with ludicrous ideas because she didn't have all the facts. All she had to do was fill-in the details—which surely were far more mundane than knickknacks flying through the perfumed air, or sad ghosts trapped in a house seeking vengeance or justice. Once she did that, her worries about spirits would vanish into thin air.

Angie headed over to the *San Francisco Chronicle's* "morgue" of old newspapers and did a search on Eric and Natalie Fleming's deaths. The *Chronicle* loved to fill news stories with personal details. Also, if there had been anything odd about the deaths the *Chronicle* would have covered them in gory detail.

She was right.

For the first time, she saw what Eric and Natalie Fleming looked like.

Eric was a very late 1970's to early 1980's looking guy with curly brown hair that hung below his ears and a broad mustache. He was also handsome enough to have been a rock star. His cheekbones were pronounced, his nose high and straight, his mouth pleasant, but his eyes most captivated her. They were remarkable, with beautifully shaped eyebrows over heavy-lidded hazel eyes. Bedroomy. Being haunted by this guy didn't seem like such a horrible proposition.

Natalie was surprisingly thin and lacking in curves. Her pale blond hair looked silky as it flowed in soft waves to her shoulders. In sharp contrast to Eric's casual jeans-clad appearance, in the newspaper photo she wore an expensive looking dress with simple yet tasteful gold and diamond jewelry.

The type of woman Joy perfume would appeal to.

Angie pushed thoughts about perfume from her mind and returned to the news articles.

Eric came from a middle class family, studied computer programing at UC Berkeley, and became one of many new "Silicon Valley millionaires" of that era.

The *Chronicle* had called Natalie an "heiress." She had been born Natalie Parker, and raised in Connecticut. Her parents had been killed when their yacht capsized in a storm off the Bahamas. Natalie, their only child, inherited their money. Family arguments over the money caused Natalie to turn her back on the remaining Parker clan and move to the West Coast.

Their bodies had been found when a neighbor's beagle ran off and refused to come back. The neighbor had no choice but to cross the Flemings' unfenced back yard to get to the dog. They might have lain there even longer had he not found them since neither Eric nor Natalie worked or had appointments that would have caused someone to look for them. Angie suspected that in those pre-cell phone, pretext message days, unanswered calls weren't cause for immediate concern.

When the owner of the home that the Flemings rented unlocked it for the police, they found two half-empty martini glasses on the bar between the kitchen and dining area. Also, two uncooked pork chops were rotting on the countertop next to a frying pan and bottle of canola oil, and lettuce, carrots, and onion lay on the countertop beside a salad bowl. Easy listening music played on KSFO, the "The Sound of the City" station.

Everything suggested that the Flemings had been interrupted while having before-dinner drinks. It didn't look at all like the kitchen of a couple fighting so bitterly that they would soon both be dead.

The biggest mystery, the thing that most caused the police to question the murder-suicide scenario, was that the couple's car was missing.

Eric Fleming drove a Mercedes 350-SL, a two-seater. Angie had learned from Paavo that the car turned up a year later in Sonoma County. She searched the newspapers to learn more about its discovery, but apparently the news editors had lost interest in the case by then. No one bothered to report that the car had been found.

In fact, only one follow-up story had been written about the deaths. It was about Natalie's small dog and how it spent every day out on the cliff as if waiting for Natalie to return. People tried to take it home and make it their own, but the dog would always find a way to escape and go back to the cliff. The paper told a brief but heartwarming story of how the neighbors worked together to assure it had food, water, and shelter from the rain.

Angie made photocopies of the most fact-filled newspaper stories.

She then went to the county assessor's office to find the history of ownership of the house on Clover Lane. A couple named Donald and Mary Steed built in the 1950's. Their son, Edward, inherited it in 1970, upon his widowed mother's death. He died in 1978, and ownership transferred to his wife, Carol. Angie could find no change in ownership after that.

Angie had found out quite a bit about Eric and Natalie's life and death, but she still had no idea why they died, or who could possibly have been responsible.

Paavo and Yosh returned to Wyndom's apartment to go through her personal and financial papers to see if any red flags jumped out at him. Her death and Bedford's had to be connected, but how? Normally, the first person they suspected was the wronged wife, but Larina Bedford seemed to care so little about Taylor they couldn't imagine her having enough feeling about him to kill him. She seemed more the type to file for divorce and enjoy taking him for every penny he had.

Scouring Gaia's tax papers, Paavo discovered she owned property in a small town on the Pacific coast highway called Jenner, some thirty miles from Healdsburg. With that, things began to click.

While Yosh went off to Zygog to follow a thin lead on Taylor, Paavo drove back to the motel in Healdsburg. He showed the desk manager he'd spoken to earlier a photo of Gaia Wyndom.

"Yes," the manager said. "That's the woman. She would pick Mr. Bedford up. I'm sorry to hear he's dead. His wife has a nice smile."

Paavo drove out to Jenner to see Gaia's house. He found it in a heavily forested spot among a row of similar cabins about a quarter mile from the beach.

The cabin was small but well maintained, brown in color, with white window frames and a red door.

No one answered his knock. Paavo went to a similar home next door where an elderly man stood outside raking leaves.

Ray Larson owned the cabin and lived there year round. Paavo asked him about the owners of the house next door.

"A single lady named Gaia Wyndom owns it," Larson said. "Met her when I bought this place some eight years ago. Guess she inherited it from her parents quite a few years back. I had the impression it didn't mean much to her. She rarely used to show up. Once a year at most. The last few months, though, her twin sister and her husband have been coming here just about every weekend."

"Her twin sister?" Paavo had found no indication anywhere that Gaia had any living relative, let alone a twin.

"Marilee, her name is. Gave me a start when I saw her. Spitting image of Gaia. Husband's name is Trevor. Nice couple. Good to see middle-aged folks in love that way."

"So, had Gaia ever mentioned having a twin or any sibling before you met her?" Paavo asked.

"Not a word." Larson seemed lost in thought a moment, then gave a little chuckle. "It was eerie, the more I think about it. Sometimes I called her Gaia by mistake, and she always answered. She said identical twins get used to that. But when you look close, you see a difference. Not physically, but in the eyes, the light from the eyes. Gaia is a serious, quiet woman with dull eyes. Marilee laughs and talks a lot. Her eyes are so bright if I didn't know better, I'd say she was downright pretty." His cheeks reddened at that. "Oh, sorry. I guess that isn't nice to say, but any fellow knows those gals weren't ones to turn a man's head, kinda plain and chubby, to my way of thinking. Still, at times, I felt sorry for Gaia. Marilee is the person she should have been."

"Do you happen to know Marilee and Trevor's last names?"

He thought a minute. "You know, I don't think they ever said. We're pretty much all on a first name basis out here, and they never got any mail or anything. The only mail that ever showed up was for Gaia, and Marilee said she'd give it to her."

"So, Marilee and Trevor lived in San Francisco?"

"I suppose. Or the two gals saw each other a lot."

"You said Marilee and Trevor showed up here every weekend?"

"They'd arrive Friday night, and leave Sunday. Not every week through. In fact, I figured out their pattern—guess I got too much time on my hands." Larson's eyes twinkled as he gave his information. "Three weekends here, one weekend not. Oh—and on the first and third weekend, they'd arrive separately, in separate cars on Friday. On the middle weekend, they'd arrive together."

Paavo nodded. That middle weekend was when Gaia picked Taylor up in Healdsburg. "When did you last see them?"

"That's easy, weekend before this past one. In fact, come to think of it, something odd happened. They left on Saturday, not Sunday like usual."

Paavo opened the folder he carried and took out a photo of Taylor Bedford. "Is this Trevor?"

The neighbor needed no time to respond. "Yes! That's him. Why do you have his picture? Can you tell me what this is about?"

Paavo hesitated only a moment. "I'm investigating his murder. His, and Gaia Wyndom's." Just to be sure, he showed Larson Gaia's photo. "That's her, right?"

"Yes, of course." Larson's bushy eyebrows rose as he looked up at Paavo. "But what about Marilee? My god, is she all right?"

"We'll check into it," Paavo said. "One question—did you ever see Gaia and Marilee together?"

"Well...no, but I'm sure there are two of them, if that's what you're thinking. No one could be that good an actress."

"Thank you." Paavo handed Larson his card. "If anyone at all shows up here please call me immediately any time of the day or night."

"I'm sorry to hear they're dead," Larson said as he took the card. "Doesn't make much sense that it would be Gaia who was killed with Trevor and not Marilee."

"That's true," Paavo agreed. "It's all quite strange, in fact."

Ray Larson nodded, and then faced the trees, his eyes growing misty. "Gaia was a nice person."

"So everyone says."

Chapter 14

PAAVO IMMEDIATELY CONTACTED Yosh with the news that Gaia either had a twin sister, or used the name Marilee to hide her relationship with Taylor Bedford. Yosh included questions about Gaia possibly having a sister to his list as he spoke with co-workers of both Taylor and Gaia.

Paavo headed back to homicide where he searched under the name "Marilee Wyndom." No one by that name appeared in any database. He tried various spellings such as "Mary Lee," "Merilee," even "Merry Lee" but nothing worked.

He then returned to Gaia's home and canvassed her neighbors to ask if any of them ever saw or heard of a sister. He basically wanted to assure himself that no sister, identical or otherwise, existed. He suspected Gaia had made up the name, just as Taylor called himself Trevor. It made sense that the two used false names to cover up their affair. Between Taylor's marriage and possible workplace non-fraternization issues, they decided to keep the relationship a secret.

To his surprise, a neighbor said she once saw the two women together, well over a year ago, and they looked almost identical except for hairstyle and that one seemed prettier than the other, perhaps because she wore some make-up and styled her hair better. Paavo tried to shake her belief in what she might have seen, but could not. The neighbor was in her thirties, a stay-at-home mother, and her vision seemed to be a solid twenty-twenty. Paavo could find, however, no one to corroborate her sighting.

So, the question was, should he believe Ray Larson and that one neighbor...or not?

Angie got a call from her sister Maria who wanted to know why Angie had asked their mother about ghosts and spirits. Angie listened to her with a sinking feeling in the pit of her stomach. Maria had also talked to Caterina and learned Angie was house-hunting, which was something else she wanted to hear about.

Maria then invited her to lunch at the Rose Tattoo restaurant on Columbus Avenue in San Francisco's North Beach district.

Angie almost said "no," but that made her feel guilty, so she agreed.

Maria was the sister she got along with the least. Well, no, that wasn't exactly true. She probably got along least well with Frannie who was just a little older than her. They used to fight all the time growing up, and continued to fight into adulthood. But then she also didn't get along all that well with Caterina until she went to Italy with her and the two of them had several heart-to-hearts. Come to think of it, the only one she never fought with was Bianca, the oldest of the lot, and the most motherly. Despite all that, she loved her sisters dearly, and was always ready to defend them if needed.

She changed into an Emilio Pucci silk dress, and drove

to the restaurant.

She knew why Maria was interested. Maria thought of herself as having "a spiritual nature." Angie thought of her as downright spooky. When Maria was a teenager, everyone in the family assumed she would become a nun. But then she met a jazz trumpet player, Dominic Klee, and married him after a whirlwind courtship. A stranger couple, Angie had never come across...unless she considered Frannie and Seth who should have gotten divorced ten times over by now. Caterina and Bianca's marriages were fine—but those sisters were both older and set in their ways. Angie couldn't imagine either of them even looking at another man. They were both nauseatingly comfortable with their spouses—sort of like not throwing away favorite slippers just because you found a new pair on sale.

In her opinion, she and Paavo were the perfect couple.

Angie gave a sad sigh for her sisters that none of them had managed to find anyone half as simultaneously cool and hot as Paavo. It seemed to take forever for her to convince him that they could be a couple, let alone get married, and yet he still made her toes tingle, her pulse quicken and her heart thrum. They came from very different backgrounds; she had a large and loving family, and he had no one but an elderly Finnish gentleman who raised him. The love he received from Aulis Kokkonen never took away the loneliness or sense of abandonment he had experienced as a child. Angie vowed he would never feel lonely or abandoned again—not as long as she had a breath left in her.

Maria stood on the sidewalk waiting for her. She was the 'exotic' Amalfi sister, with long, straight black hair, olive skin, and dark brown eyes. She liked to dress in deeply colored, gauzy clothes, and enjoyed turquoise and silver jewelry. Paavo once said—to Angie's irritation—that Maria was exceptionally beautiful. Men's taste could be quite mysterious.

After the two finished with small talk and gave their orders to the waitress, Maria took a sip of her Cabernet Sauvignon and then turned her nearly black eyes on Angie. "Okay, little sister, I know you didn't talk to Mamma about ghosts because you've developed an interest in the afterlife. What crazy thing is going on with you this time?"

Angie bit her tongue to avoid giving the answer the tone of that question deserved. Angie sipped some merlot because biting her tongue hadn't helped. Finally, she said, "I found a house that Paavo and I both love and can afford, but it sometimes has a strange ambiance to it. And I just found out it hasn't been lived in for thirty years."

Maria gawked at her. "Thirty years? You're joking! I wouldn't want to buy a house that no one has lived in that long. It could be infested with rats and heaven only knows what else. Where is this dump?"

"The Sea Cliff."

"No way! It must be falling apart because of an earthquake or something."

"Not according to Cat. The former owner maintained it well, and now her daughter wants her to sell it."

Maria gave a toss of the head. "There's your first problem: believing anything Cat says where money is involved." Maria then contorted her face into one of those piously angelic expressions that made Angie want to hit her with a cream pie as she added, "She knows nothing about what is truly valuable in the world."

"That's Cat for you," Angie said.

"Did she show you any other houses?"

"About a hundred." Angie stopped talking as the waitress brought them orders of spinach, mushroom, ricotta cheese frittata, and a chicken Caesar salad, which they proceeded to split between them.

After a few bites of the frittata, Angie continued, "Aside from all that, whenever anyone tries to buy the house I like, they back out of the deal for one reason or another."

Maria's brows rose at this. "Cut to the chase, Angie. What's going on?"

"The last people who lived there—tenants not owners—were murdered." At Maria's horrified expression, she quickly added, "Not in the house, but near it. It looked like the husband shot his wife and then himself. The police questioned that conclusion, but could find no evidence that both had been murdered. Questions remained, including their car being stolen and not found for a year miles from San Francisco. The case remains unresolved to this day."

Angie then told Maria all she had learned about the deceased occupants. At the end of her tale, Maria sat silently for a moment, then exclaimed, "You've got to show me this house right now!"

Angie insisted that Maria not tell Cat about Angie's key to the house. Maria agreed; she would have agreed to just about anything to get inside it.

Even as she opened the door, Angie thought this was not a good idea.

Maria remained on the front porch and made the sign of the cross before stepping across the threshold into the house.

"Ooooh," she said, as she slowly moved to the center of the living room, her arms wide and her hands raised as if she were holding a beach ball on her head. "It feels cold in here. Very, very cold."

"Well, the heater hasn't been on in some time." Angie said, dismayed, but hoping this would be as bad as it got. "And the house is on the ocean so the breeze is fairly brisk."

Maria lowered her hands and turned in a circle. "Someone is here."

Oh, God! "Someone?" Angie asked.

"Or something," Maria whispered.

"This was a bad mistake!" Angie said. "We should leave."

Maria suddenly turned pale and gripped Angie's arm. "Something feels off."

"Off?" Angie repeated.

Maria clasped her hands together and pressed them to her chest. "Oh, my, this is so terrible," she said, although her voice said it was exciting and wonderful. "When something feels bad in the house, it usually means there are *evil spirits.*" Her voice now dropped and she inched closer to Angie. "Dark beings who want to do you harm!"

"No way!" Angie stepped back and shook her head. Truth be told, her whole body shook at Maria's wild-eyed gaze. She wasn't sure if her nerves crackled because of the house or her crazy sister. "I don't think that's the case."

Maria slowly turned her head so far to one side she reminded Angie of the first time she watched Linda Blair in the old movie, *The Exorcist*. At least Maria's head wasn't spinning...yet. "Someone is living here," Maria whispered.

"You think that because the house is furnished." Angie was frantic. "Even Connie said it looks like the owners could come walking in."

Maria's gaze fixed on Angie. "Have you ever noticed

any emanations?"

"Eman—"

"Something moving, or from the corner of your eye see something zip past, or notice a scent in the air that shouldn't be there."

Angie was near tears. "Yes...yes...and yes."

Maria tucked in her chin. "Surely, you know what's going on."

"No." The word came out as a squawk

Maria looked heavenward and heaved a sigh before continuing. "Look, the Flemings are connected to the house because this is where they wanted to live their lives. They expected fun, *life!* But instead, someone stole their lives, someone who may still be alive, and unpunished." She folded her arms, eyebrows raised. "My guess is that's why the house is haunted."

"Just stop!" Angie covered her ears. "I do *not* want to hear that the house I want to buy is haunted!"

Maria tugged on Angie's arms, trying to free her ears so Angie would listen to her. Angie slapped her hands away.

Maria moved closer and shouted, "THE SIMPLEST REASON FOR SOMETHING HAPPENING IS MOST OFTEN THE CORRECT ONE. THAT THIS HOUSE IS HAUNTED IS THE MOST DIRECT EXPLANATION!"

"No it's not!" Angie lowered her hands realizing nothing could block out the sound of Maria's shrieks. "Ghosts don't exist!"

"Not in your world," Maria gave one of her all-knowing, oh-so-superior smiles. "But in mine, there are a lot of them."

Angie counted to ten. "All right, since you know all, tell me what to do about them. How do I get rid of them? If such things exist, of course."

Maria pondered Angie's questions. "You know, Angie, this could be very interesting."

"I don't want interesting!" Angie put her hands to her forehead and turned in a circle. "I want dull. I want normal!" She raised her arms to the ceiling, head back. "Other people can buy a house and not have to worry about it being haunted, why can't I?"

"Stop the dramatics and listen to me!" Maria leaned closer, her dark eyes twinkling with macabre interest. "You might want to find out why they're here."

"They?"

"Oh, yes. I'm sure there's more than one spirit here."

"You mean they're having some sort of a convention? My God!"

"Stop shrieking! You're making my ears ring. It's not that bad. Lots of houses are haunted. People learn to ignore what they see and can't explain, and develop completely wrong explanations for that which they can't ignore."

Angie flung herself onto the sofa. "So the best thing for me to do is to ignore everything."

Maria sat beside her. "Of course not! If you leave things as they are, who knows what will happen? If the spirits here are dark ones, you could become possessed!"

"Possessed?" Angie felt as if her throat closed simply trying to get the word out.

"I don't expect you to know how to deal with such things," Maria said.

"You've got that right," Angie said, worried now. "How do I do it?"

Maria pressed her palms together, her face beaming. "It's easy," she announced, looking happier than Angie had seen her in a long, long time. "Why didn't I think of this earlier? It's the answer to everything. We'll hold an exorcism!"

Chapter 15

PAAVO AND YOSH compared notes and discovered neither had gotten very far in the investigation. Yosh talked to everyone at Zygog about Gaia and Bedford. He had the clear impression that Gaia had been attracted to Bedford for a number of years, but in the past month or so, people noticed that when he wandered near, Gaia would rush away. In the past, she would stare at him with round cow eyes, and hang onto his every word like a puppy.

No one thought much of it because Otto Link had made it clear to everyone that he and his boss were an item. Link had the plushest job in the place since Bedford spent two weeks out of town each month, and during those days Link had little work to do. He read books and played computer games. No one dared to complain since they feared Link would accuse them of homophobia.

The more Yosh looked into it, the more he began to suspect Otto Link's affair took place more in his mind than in fact.

Bedford's wife was the mystery. If his marriage was as dysfunctional as Otto Link and the weekend rendezvous with Gaia—or her mysterious sister—made it appear, why did she put up with it? From all he could tell, she lived a life completely separate from Bedford's. She had her own circle of friends and organizations that she belonged to. Her days were busy, and she didn't seem to care if she had male companionship or not. When Bedford was in town, he escorted her to functions; when he wasn't, she went with other people.

Perhaps the saddest thing in this case, to Yosh, was that Gaia was so alone in the world that no one claimed her body. In fact, her boss, Julio Sanchez, was the only person they could find to go to the morgue to identify her. She had made no provisions for burial, which meant she would most likely be cremated by the state. It was a dismal end to what had appeared to be a lonely life until Bedford entered it. And now he was gone...perhaps by her hand.

Yosh wanted to think that Larina Bedford had killed both of them—she had motive, and she was distinctly unlikable. But if she had murdered them, she may have committed the perfect crime because they couldn't find one shred of evidence against her.

Paavo read over the M.E.'s preliminary report. "You know, Yosh," he said, "the time of death for Gaia is all over the map, but we know she was still alive after Bedford's murder."

"I've been thinking about that, too," Yosh said. "When I talked to the bartender, he said something had upset Bedford about his relationship with the mystery woman. What if something happened between them, and that something split them apart? Maybe Gaia, who never had anyone at all in her life, couldn't stand to lose him."

"So you're leaning towards her killing him and then committing suicide?" Paavo asked.

"Stranger things have happened."

"We've got to figure out if there really is a twin sister,"

Paavo said. "That'll be the key."

"There's no evidence of it," Yosh insisted.

"Except for one neighbor and one old man who believed there really were two different women."

"Or one sad woman who finally found somebody who made her happy," Yosh said.

Paavo couldn't let the idea of a twin go. He talked to her neighbors again, asking if they ever saw her on weekends. None could remember with certainly, except that they rarely saw her at any time. She had a car but she always had it in the garage when she in or out.

Then an idea struck. He knew Gaia's date and place of birth, and drove to each hospital in Oakland, California until he found the one with a hospital record of her birth. Looking at the record, he learned that Shirley Wyndom had, in fact, given birth to twin girls forty-four years earlier. The girls were named Gaia Ann and Urda Lee.

With this starting point, back in homicide, he tracked the girls to Marin County where their parents moved when they were eight years old. He followed their schooling through graduation from Drake High in San Anselmo.

Both parents were killed five days after the girls' twenty-first birthday when their car ran off the road on Highway 1 just south of Jenner. Their assets went to their two daughters.

After that, he found no further mention of Urda. He could find no Social Security number for her, no California Driver's License number or any other normal part of life. He could find no evidence that she paid taxes or died. It was most peculiar.

The Jenner house was in Gaia's name only.

So what had happened to her sister? Was she, or was Gaia, the woman called Marilee?

Paavo expanded his search to extended family members. Surely, someone existed who remembered those girls.

"Maria wants an exorcism, but she can't get one," Angie said to Connie over shrimp salads at a Fisherman's Wharf restaurant. Since Paavo was working on his murder investigation that evening, Angie decided it would be a good time to talk to her best friend.

Connie choked on a shrimp. "You're joking."

"You've met Maria," Angie said. "She never jokes. I no sooner let her into the house than she went all 'woo-woo' on me, and said I could become possessed if we buy it."

"Good God!" Connie gasped. "Why in heaven's name did you take her there?"

"She wanted to see it. I thought it'd be harmless. No such luck."

"So now she's trying to get an exorcism for you?"

"None of the priests she knows—and she knows a lot of them—will go to the Bishop about providing an exorcist unless there's some outward sign of a person being possessed. They can't do an exorcism on a house just because someone 'thinks' a ghost might live there. They told Maria she's jumping the gun."

"Or jumping the shark," Connie said. "Maybe the whole fish tank."

"If only another house would come up, I'd forget this one," Angie said, eating as if the food were cardboard. "But none of the affordable ones are half so nice."

"Look, honey, Maria is ridiculous! Ignore her."

"But even you said it felt odd." Angie took her napkin off her lap and put it on the table. She had no more appetite. "I don't know what to do."

"It felt odd because it stood empty for so long, that's all." Connie stabbed one of Angie's crouton's with her fork. Her appetite was fine.

"But now that I've got Maria thinking the place is haunted, she'll tell Mamma, and my mother will be afraid to come visit me!"

"Would your mother believe the house is haunted?" Connie asked.

"In a heartbeat."

Connie thought a moment. "So the only problem now is your sister's involvement."

"No. My problem is that bargain-hunter's House of Dark Shadows," Angie cried.

Connie remembered her conversation with Stan, how he worried that Angie had not only become obsessed with the house, but it caused her to possibly believe in ghosts. Stan thought it best if she forgot about that house and stayed in her apartment. Connie hated to admit that Stan could be right, but he was.

With that, inspiration struck. Even Connie was amazed that such a crazy and frankly devious idea had come to her. Angie usually came up with ideas like that.

Connie cleared her throat to get Angie's full attention. "Well, it's not Catholic at all, but it might work on Maria," she began. "I know a woman who's dabbled in the occult and performs séances."

"A séance?" Angie interrupted. "Maria won't believe in a séance!"

"This woman has acted on stage, and she's quite good. Her séances feel very real, trust me on that!"

Angie shook her head. "I don't think—"

"Just listen. We'll invite Maria to the house and hold a séance. My friend will tell Maria the ghosts have gone. That way, you'll have Maria off your back, and you can think about buying the house with a clear head."

Angie thought a moment. "If your friend can pull it off, that actually is a good idea."

Connie smiled slyly.

The next day, Paavo tracked down a second cousin of the twin girls' father, Henry Wyndom. She was eighty years old, living in Los Angeles. After a conversation by phone that convinced him she had information, he went to Lt. Eastwood and got approval to catch the next commuter plane to L.A.

Helen Atherton was a bright, well-turned out woman. She invited Paavo into her pleasant but cluttered home.

"I really can't tell you much about Gaia. I'm sorry to hear she's dead, but I haven't seen her or her sister in years," she said even before Paavo sat down in the living room. She offered him coffee or tea, and put out some vanilla wafers. He gladly accepted a cup of coffee. She soon sat down across from him, ready to answer questions.

"You mentioned Gaia's sister," Paavo began. "Was there only one? No brothers?"

"One sister, a twin. That was all; and that was enough if you ask me." She gave a firm nod. "I had nothing to do with the girls after their parents died, I'm sorry to admit. I just never cared for them."

"What can you tell me about their parents' deaths?"

"Not much except that their car apparently went out of control on Highway 1 on the way home from their cabin in Jenner. It ran off the road and rolled down a cliff along the Pacific."

Her wording struck him. Also, being face-to-face with her convinced him her mind was sharp and her words honest. "You said it 'apparently' went out of control?"

"That's right. That road twists like the Dickens, but my cousin knew it well. I'm not saying accidents don't happen, but Henry was a very careful driver. If anything, he drove too slow! And Henry always maintained his cars. I see no reason for it to have gone off the highway, unless someone helped it along."

Interesting speculation, Paavo thought. "Were you and Henry close?"

"As children we were. But I didn't care for his wife, Shirley, so I saw less and less of them as time went on."

"The twins were age twenty-one when their parents died, so I take it they inherited everything?" Paavo asked.

"They certainly did, including a house in Kentfield. It was pricey when Henry and Shirley bought it in the 1970's, but worth a small fortune when the girls finally decided to sell it a few years back. They must have made a tidy sum off the place, even splitting it between them."

"What do you think really happened to their parents?"

"I have no idea. It was called 'driver error.' The car caught fire, so there wasn't really much left to investigate, I suppose. And no reason to suspect anything. No real reason, in any case."

"Meaning?"

She pursed her lips, then sat up a little straighter. "Meaning I always found it suspicious that their parents died shortly after, as adults, those two could take charge of their inheritance. To me, those girls had ice water in their veins. They didn't even hold a funeral service or anything for their parents. I doubt they ever shed a tear for them. They were little demons when they were growing up, and I doubt they were any better as adults." She raised her head. "I wouldn't put anything past either one of them And I'd never turn my back on them, either."

Paavo turned the conversation to the missing twin. "Gaia lived in San Francisco and worked in South San Francisco before she died. But I can find nothing about Urda. As far as you know, is she still alive? Any idea where she might be living?"

"I know Urda is alive because I see her books in stores. A new one comes out every six months or so."

He was surprised. "She's a writer?"

"Yes. Paranormal romances—werewolves and vampires, that sort of thing. She makes a fortune at it, too, I understand."

"She doesn't use the name Urda Wyndom, does she?"

"My gracious, no. She uses a pseudonym, Marilee Wisdom."

"I see," Paavo said. "Do you have any idea where she lives?"

"Urda was always a free spirit compared to Gaia. She didn't like to be tied down by many possessions. I wouldn't be surprised to learn she lived out in the woods somewhere. She used to live in Marin County, or maybe Sonoma. I doubt she'd go much farther than that. The two sisters didn't get along, but they always kept an eye on each other—a close eye. If Gaia lived in San Francisco, Urda wasn't far away."

"How well did they get along?" Paavo asked.

Helen snorted. "Like oil and water. Each always tried to get the upper hand on the other."

"Were their personalities the same or different?"

"Exactly the same. Both pretended to be nice, but they weren't. I already said they were demons as children. As adults, I wouldn't be surprised to learn they were monsters."

Paavo found the words chilling, but the more he learned about this case, the more he believed she was right.

He handed her his card, thanked her for her time, and left.

Chapter 16

ANGIE OPENED THE apartment door to find two women making tiny waving gestures and smiling at her.

"Hello, we're from Bride's Little Helpers." They spoke at the same time, and it was like listening in stereo. After not liking the pushy, opinionated wedding planners she met, Angie decided to move in a completely different direction and contacted a firm that described their services as providing assistance in the planning of a wedding, and fulfilling the bride's every dream. She contacted them that morning and, to her amazement, they said they would be there in an hour. And they were.

The two looked nothing alike beyond their blond hair, blue eyes, and too much red lipstick. Angie showed them to her living room as they oohed and aahed over her lovely apartment and view that stretched from the Golden Gate Bridge across the north bay and Alcatraz all the way to the Bay Bridge. Angie cringed as they headed towards her Cezanne but they either didn't know the artist or didn't care about the lithograph because they continued past it without a word.

They sat on the sofa and Angie took the yellow

Hepplewhite chair.

"I'm Lara," the one on the right said.

"And I'm Kara," said the one on the left.

"We do everything you don't want to bother with. You simply tell us what you want and we'll do it, just like magic!" Lara said, brimming with enthusiasm.

"And we're always Johnny-on-the-spot," Kara said, her little fist punching the air.

"That's why we came here so soon after you called," Lara added.

"It shows our dedication," said Kara.

"And consideration of you..." Lara waited for Kara to join in, as both added, "and your time."

Angie blinked a moment. "You see, I'm not sure what I want or need." She looked from one to the other. "That's why I'm hiring a wedding assistant. I mean, I know the basics, but it's the details I worry about."

"That's what we're here for. Details. You just tell us what you want done, and we'll do it," Lara repeated, clapping her hands.

Next, Kara showed how over-the-top bubbly she could be. "Don't worry, you'll think of everything eventually. Our brides always do, don't they, Lara?" Both nodded and smiled so broadly Angie could see their molars.

"But do you offer help or suggestions?" Angie asked.

"We can, but for some reason most of our brides don't seem to like that, no they don't." Lara glanced at Kara and both women shook their heads vehemently.

"They want us to do what they want us to do, nothing more, nothing less," Kara chimed, forcefully jabbing her forefinger on Angie's coffee table.

Lara folded her hands together. "And that's what we do. That's why we're..."

Suddenly the two hooked arms, leaned their heads towards each other and sang out, *"Briiides little hellllpers!"*

Angie gawked. She was already getting a crick in her neck going back and forth from one person to the other. No way in hell could she tolerate these two over the next four months. She stood and tried to sound calm as she said, "I'll call you."

Angie shut the door on them and returned to her sofa where she sat and miserably stared at the far wall. The one that was empty. No Cezanne, no nothing. Just like her wedding.

What was wrong with her? She couldn't find anyone she liked to help with her wedding; she couldn't find a house for Paavo and her to live in that wasn't potentially haunted; and she hadn't even found a wedding dress. Was her taste so completely out of step with the rest of the world? Other people found wedding planners; other people found houses to buy.

Other people found jobs they managed to keep!

Why couldn't she?

Angie wasn't the only one agonizing about life choices and the future. Paavo's involvement with the dysfunctional Wyndom family caused him to think about and fret over the upcoming changes to his life.

He, who had never really had a family, would soon become part of an enormous one. He had to admit he found it somewhat horrifying.

But most horrifying of all was the wedding Angie planned. It sounded like a cross between "My Big Fat Greek Wedding" and the battle scenes from "Saving Private Ryan." It was enough to give a 6'2", 180 lb., strong and tough death cop palpitations.

He left Homicide early and went straight to Angie's apartment.

Angie opened the door and greeted Paavo with a kiss. He set her from him and stepped backwards, his expression troubled. "Angie, I've been thinking."

She stiffened as a thousand possibilities of what could be wrong flooded her mind, starting with *"Stan was right! He's going to call off the wedding!"*

He continued. "Isn't it going to be a bit weird to have a wedding with so many people from your family, and my side of the church has no one but Aulis? Why don't we let your side have the whole church and let Aulis sit with your parents?"

She blinked a couple of times. *Is that all?* "I don't think your side will be that empty, but that'll be fine. I wouldn't want Aulis to feel alone."

"Good," he said with a nod.

She knew there was something more, and expected it might be a subject they had put off talking about. But the time had come for her to broach it. "Since we're on the subject of the wedding," she said, "have you chosen your best man yet?"

He shook his head, walked over to the sofa, and eased himself onto it. She understood the problem—the person he wanted, Matt Kowalski, was dead. He also told her Matt's wife had started dating. Life went on, but sometimes it was much more difficult than others.

She sat beside him. He once said he thought loneliness preferable to loss. He had suffered too many losses in his life, and she watched how, after Matt's death, he never allowed himself to grow close to anyone else in the homicide bureau. With his job keeping him busy, he had little time to socialize and make friends outside the force. It was, frankly, amazing he was engaged.

She took his hand. "Yosh?" she suggested.

"We're partners and I like him a lot, but we rarely see each other outside work. He might feel odd being a best man because of that. If I ask, he might want to say 'no' but feel stuck. The whole thing could be uncomfortable."

"What about Calderon? You always seemed to like him."

"Calderon hates weddings, and hates marriages."

"But he enjoys talking to my sister, Frannie, I've heard," Angie said with a wry smile followed by a shudder.

"I couldn't ask Calderon instead of Yosh," Paavo said. "That wouldn't work at all. Yosh would be hurt. We should ask both to the wedding, although I doubt either will come."

Angie thought he was wrong about that, but said nothing.

"What about Cat's husband?" Paavo asked. "We got along well when we went to Rome together."

"Charles? But he's so boring! We'd have to hold a mirror under his nose to make sure he's alive. Besides, he has to walk Cat down the aisle since she'll be a bridesmaid."

"Can't Stan walk her?"

"Why not make Stan your best man?" Angie suggested. "That way he'll have a role in the wedding."

Paavo didn't even respond to that. Okay, even she had to admit that was a stretch.

Paavo looked despondent. "I never realized I'm such a loner," he said. "My work has taken over my life, cutting out friendships. I've got to do something about that."

Angie wracked her brain; seeing her groom so

unhappy hurt. "Who do you talk to at work?"

"Yosh, mainly. And Rebecca. Say, shouldn't Rebecca be in the wedding somewhere?"

Angie thought about his tall, buxom, beautiful co-worker; the one who wanted to marry Paavo herself; the one—she had been told—everyone in homicide thought was perfect for him. Angie would feel as if she were standing in a hole if Rebecca were in the wedding party. She could just imagine Paavo looking right over her head into Rebecca's big blue adoring eyes. The idea was horrible!

"That's not going to work. I've got way too many sisters to have room for anybody else. It's only through juggling that Connie fits in as my maid (or matron, since she was once married) of honor. And she's my best friend!"

"Well...maybe I can find myself some friends before you finalize the wedding line-up," Paavo said more dejected than ever. She had no idea this wedding would put such a strain on him.

Chapter 17

STAN, YOU WERE right," Connie said into the phone the next morning. She was bursting with excitement over her clever idea, and couldn't wait to share it.

"What am I right about?"

Connie could hear that he sounded sleepy. "Did I wake you up? It's eleven o'clock. Are you sick?"

"No. I just didn't feel like going to work today. I've got a lot on my mind with Angie's wedding and all. I worried so much about who my new neighbor will be once she moves, I must have dozed off again."

"I'm calling about Angie, so wake up and listen to me!" Connie said. "It's important!"

"Let's go back to me being right," Stan muttered.

"Angie is going too far with this house business. She's hardly rational. She told me her sister Maria wanted to have an exorcism done on the house, and Angie doesn't even realize how crazy that sounds! She's losing it, Stan. Too much pressure between house-hunting and the wedding. We need to help her."

"An exorcism? Are you joking?"

"No, but at least it's not going to happen. I've got an idea, however, about something that can happen. I know a woman who performs séances. I called her and she's available tonight."

"A séances sounds even goofier than an exorcism," Stan said. "I don't want anything to do with a séance! You're more insane than Angie!"

"Me? You're the one who's the spoils sport!" Connie spat out the words. "My idea is perfect! I'll get Angie to hold a séance with Madame Hermione, and invite her sister Maria to attend. Now, here's where it gets clever. Angie will think Madame Hermione is there to convince Maria that the house isn't haunted, but in fact, she'll do the *opposite*. She'll act like it is! That way, Angie will be forced to drop the whole idea of buying a house that scares her."

"And she just might stay in her apartment," Stan said hopefully.

"For a little while, at least. Anyway, I think we're on the same page," Connie said. "Now, you and I need to meet with Hermione this afternoon. She'll brief you on scary 'ghostlike' things to do. I think if you hide outside in the back yard and work with Hermione to make noises and what have you, it'll appear that she's conjuring up spirits. Then she'll announce that the house really is haunted, and Angie will drop any ideas about buying it!"

"Yeah, but what am I supposed to do to sound like a ghost?"

"You can take some heavy chains. Don't ghosts rattle them? And bring a horn with a low, deep sound."

"A horn? I don't...oh, I played clarinet in middle school for a couple of months. What should I blow on it?"

Connie looked heavenward for strength. "Anything, Stan! Who cares? What about the 'Dies Irae' theme?"

"I don't know how it goes."

"Find anything that makes noise or flashes lights. It

doesn't matter what. It's the thought that counts."

Stan remained quiet. "Stan?" she called.

"I'm here. I was hoping I could go back to sleep so when I woke up, I'd find this was all a terrible dream."

Early that afternoon, Paavo and Yosh pulled onto the driveway belonging to Urda Wyndom, aka Marilee Wisdom.

Once Paavo learned she might be living in Marin County, he tracked her to Lagunitas, a small community surrounded by park land and redwood forest preserves.

Urda Lee Wyndom had legally changed her name to Marilee Wisdom when she was only twenty-two years old. Paavo looked up the proceedings for the name change. She petitioned the court saying being stuck with "Urda" the rest of her life should be considered cruel and unusual punishment. The judge agreed.

Paavo had worked cases before where someone had their name legally changed, but records of the earlier name had always remained on the books. New records came into being, but the old ones hadn't been deleted. Not in this case, however. He had no idea how she had pulled that off, but somehow she had.

Adding to the strangeness, Paavo found Urda—or Marilee as she was now known—had a completely made-up biography on her website and Facebook page claiming Marilee was British and lived in London, of all places. He supposed she claimed friendship with J.K. Rowling as well. Everything about her seemed to be imaginary.

Yet, even knowing this, he found it startling to see a person open the door who so greatly resembled the picture of the corpse he had on the murder board facing his desk. Even their hairstyles were the same—side part, casual, chin length.

"Inspectors Smith and Yoshiwara, San Francisco P.D.," Paavo said as he and Yosh showed their badges. "Are you Marilee Wisdom?"

"Yes, I am." She looked confused. "What's this about?"

"Your sister, Gaia Wyndom. May we come in?"

She let them into the house, a small A-frame with large windows facing the forest. The interior consisted of a great room with rustic plaids, comfortable pillows, and leather and wood furnishings. It was a far cry from the sterile, stiff furniture in Gaia's home. Upstairs was a bedroom loft. Marilee picked up two gray and white cats from the back of the sofa, tossed them out to what appeared to be a covered back porch and shut the door, then invited Paavo and Yosh to sit down.

"When did you last see your sister?" Paavo asked.

Marilee shrugged. "Some weeks ago. Why?"

"Did you communicate otherwise? Texts? E-mail?"

"Sometimes. Not recently. What's this about?"

"Did she ever mention to you anyone who had threatened her, or anyone she was afraid of for any reason?"

"No. You two are scaring me. Is she all right?"

"Was there any special person in her life? Someone she may have been romantically involved with?"

Marilee's whole demeanor suddenly changed. She snorted. "Gaia? I don't think she's had a boyfriend since high school. Oh, wait." She smirked. "She didn't have any in high school either."

Marilee looked them straight in the eye as she announced, "I went to the prom, not her. Why are you asking such questions?"

Paavo glanced at Yosh, who then took over. "I'm sorry

to say, we have bad news," Yosh said, and then gently told her of Gaia's death.

Marilee showed little emotion, and what she showed was a combination of surprise and disgust. She took a deep breath then asked, "So, it was suicide?"

"That has yet to be determined," Yosh responded.

"I see."

"Is there anything in Gaia's past that would lead you to believe she might commit suicide?" Paavo asked.

"She wasn't a happy person. Lonely, I'd say."

"I'm surprised you didn't hear about her death from anyone," Paavo said. "And didn't read about it in the newspaper."

Marilee brusquely tucked a lock of hair behind an ear as if all these questions wearied her. "I don't pay attention to the news. I hate hearing or seeing anything about all the death and destruction going on in the world. I'm much happier ignoring it. The only newspaper I look at is the local one, and I'm afraid people living around me don't care about the terrible things that happen in San Francisco."

"You recently faced the death of someone else close to you," Paavo said.

Marilee stiffened. "Oh?"

"Taylor Bedford," Paavo said.

Marilee paled. "I should have expected the police would turn up information about his personal life." Her jaw clenched and her breathing became quick and shallow. "Have you learned who killed him yet?"

"We were hoping you could help us."

She looked from Paavo to Yosh. "Do you think there's a connection between his death and Gaia's? That's so hard to imagine! According to Taylor, he rarely saw her at work, and their jobs had nothing in common."

"Right now, you're the only connection between the two of them."

Her eyes widened. "Me? You think this had something to do with me?"

Paavo's expression was cold. "We were told he kept your relationship a secret. That he never even spoke about you to anyone."

"That's where you're wrong." Her tone was harsh. "He wanted to announce to the world the way he felt about me. He even pursued me at work!"

"Pursued you at work? What do you mean? You didn't work with him, your sister did."

She looked stunned a moment. "What I mean is…is that I didn't tell him for a long time that I wasn't Gaia."

"Why not?"

She folded her hands, fingers intertwined. "When we met, he thought I was Gaia. It was easier, in some ways even more exciting, if I pretended to be my twin. The poor waif, coming out of her shell thanks to the love of a rich, powerful man in her company, yada yada. I felt I was in an old Harlequin romance come to life." She chuckled. "I'm a romance writer, if you didn't know. Paranormal romances—sexy vampires, sexy shape-shifters, sexy werewolves, occasionally sexy humans. They're very popular these days, and sell remarkably well."

"And you make enough to live on?"

"More than you can imagine," she said with a cloying smile.

"I see." Paavo said. "Did you ever tell him who you were?"

"Eventually," she said.

He noticed her fingers turning white she clutched

them so tightly. "When?"

"A couple of weeks ago."

"How long ago did your affair begin?" he asked.

"I'd say, um, six months ago. In the spring."

"And all that time he thought you were Gaia?" Paavo couldn't believe that degree of deception.

"What did it matter?"

"I think it would have mattered a great deal to him."

Marilee sighed. "I'm not proud of what I did. It started out as a lark. I never dreamed I would fall in love with him."

"Go on," Paavo urged.

"I met Gaia one day after work. We walked into a nearby bar to talk about some financial stuff, but we no sooner entered than she froze. She didn't want him to see her—or us—I'm not sure which. She pointed him out as a big shot in sales and from the way she talked and stared at him, I could tell she was smitten. It made me curious."

"And then what?" Paavo asked.

"A couple of weeks later, I saw him in a grocery store, Safeway, in the Marina district. We began talking. We left the store and went out for coffee. I liked him, and we shared many interests. Once we started talking, it seemed we never stopped." A shadow crossed over her face. "Until now."

"You just happened to meet him and just happened to talk to him?"

She shrugged. "You could say that. And didn't I already say that Gaia, who never even dated, was half in love with him? I wanted to find out why."

"I assume you knew Bedford was married."

"Of course."

"Wasn't that a problem?"

"Not for me. I didn't care. Marriage means nothing to me. Neither does having children. My parents didn't have a happy marriage, Inspector. And, as I'm sure you found out since you've done so much snooping into my private life, Gaia and I do not have other close relatives. I would say the gene for procreation doesn't run in our family. I'm quite happy to be independent."

"But you said Taylor wanted to tell the world about the two of you. That must have included his wife."

"It did," she said. "Taylor didn't like 'cheating' on his wife as he put it. He was very twentieth century that way. He repeatedly asked his wife for a divorce, but she refused to agree to an amicable one. She threatened to take everything he owned if he walked out on her."

"What did you think of that?"

She shrugged. "Nothing. It was his problem, not mine."

"Why didn't you come forward, talk to the police, when you learned he had been murdered?"

"I didn't have anything to offer about who did it. And his wife would have been there. I didn't want to see her."

"Or you had something to do with his murder," Paavo said.

"Do I look like a murderer, Inspector?" Marilee asked. "I didn't kill him. I was probably the only person in the world who truly loved him."

Paavo paused a moment in the questioning. "What did Taylor say when you told him you weren't Gaia?"

"He said that explained a lot. And he didn't care. He loved me."

Paavo looked up at Yosh to see Yosh had some questions of his own. Yosh shook his head.

Paavo was ready to leave, but not before one last

question. "What do you think happened to your sister and Taylor Bedford?"

"I'm not sure I should speculate," she said.

"Try it," Paavo suggested.

"His wife knew about the affair, and I'm sure she thought it was between Taylor and Gaia. I suspected all along that she paid someone to kill Taylor. Now that I learn Gaia is dead, she probably hired someone to kill her as well. It's her style to keep her hands clean, Inspector, no matter how much shit she makes fly. Trust me on that."

By the time Paavo finished filling in Lt. Eastwood on the Marilee/Urda interview, it was early evening. Since Angie told him she was going to a 'girl's night out' with friends, Paavo decided it would be a good opportunity to pay a visit to the Night Hawk, the bar around the corner from the station where he used to work before his promotion and move to the Hall of Justice. In San Francisco, instead of each station or precinct having its own robbery, homicide, and other investigative divisions, a Bureau of Investigations had been established in the Hall of Justice. As a result, Paavo rarely saw his old co-workers.

"Hey, Paavo!" a voice called the moment he walked into the bar.

Paavo turned to see Joel Rhodes waving at him. Joel was a good guy, one he and Matt used to drink with on occasion. "Good to see you, Joel," Paavo said as they shook hands then walked up to the bar. Joel already had a beer, and Paavo ordered one.

"What are you doing slumming around here?" Joel asked with a grin.

"Just wanted to see what you guys are up to. You haven't been making trouble like usual, so I kind of lost touch."

"Yeah, it's been a while. Ever since"—Joel's voice dropped—"Matt's funeral."

"I still can't believe I won't see him again." Paavo took a sip of his beer. "But what have you been up to?"

Joel told him the latest gossip in the precinct, and Paavo talked about life in homicide, as well as Matt's widow starting to date some guy who wasn't a cop. They drank more beer, shot some pool. A couple of new cops that Paavo hadn't met before joined them. All were nice guys, but Paavo quickly realized he had no place in their lives, and they had none in his.

While he was there, feeling like a fish out of water, his phone rang. To his amazement, it was Bianca, Angie's oldest sister.

Chapter 18

A NGIE, CATERINA, AND Maria sat on the ugly green and gold sofa and equally outdated side chair in the living room of the house on Clover Lane. On the table in front of them were glasses of chardonnay, plus a bowl of plain and chocolate-covered pretzels and another of cashews.

Outside, the stars were hidden by heavy clouds, and the only sound was that of waves lapping on the beach far below.

"I don't like this," Maria muttered. "It feels like blasphemy."

"It'll be fine," Angie said, checking her watch. It was nine-fifteen; Connie was late. "Connie insists this person is quite good. Her séance will prove that the house isn't really haunted."

"It's hard to prove a negative, Angie," Maria said.

"Unless that negative has no logic or common sense," Cat said, staring daggers at Maria.

A howling wind kicked up. The lights flickered and then went out. Angie opened the front door and saw that lights were out throughout the neighborhood. The wind grew worse and it started raining. Fortunately, Angie had brought a lot of candles for the séance, and lit them now.

She hadn't thought Caterina would be here. She had only invited Maria, but then Maria phoned Cat and berated her for trying to sell Angie a haunted house. Cat told Maria she was crazy, and then phoned Bianca to complain about Maria interfering with her business. Bianca suggested Cat attend to prove Maria wrong, and so here she was.

Now the three of them sat nervously by candlelight, not saying a word. Even Angie had to confess to being a bit spooked.

Finally, the doorbell rang. Angie jumped to her feet. "That's got to be Connie!" She hurried to open the door.

Angie didn't know what to make of Connie's friend. At least she didn't show up wearing a turban, a billowy full length dress, a cape, or rows of silver necklaces like seers in the movies. She had short, frizzy hair, and wore flat sandals and a smock-like paisley print dress over a rotund figure. She towered over the Amalfi sisters. The rings she wore on each finger looked so tight, they seemed in danger of cutting off her circulation.

"No power?" Connie asked as she stepped out from behind Madame Hermione into the living room.

"It went out a few minutes ago," Angie replied.

"That makes the atmosphere even better. Let me introduce my friend." Connie made quick introductions. "Do you want to start now, Madame Hermione?"

"Let's not settle down quite yet, Connie," Hermione said. "I need to get a sense of the house, of the spirits I'm supposed to call up. Let me walk around here a bit, inside and out. And in the meantime, perhaps our hostess can put some chairs around a table."

She opened the door to the back yard and a harsh, cold wind immediately smacked her. Her hair flew back so forcefully it was almost straight, and her dress swirled around her, the hem flapping in the breeze. She quickly shut the door again. "Well, perhaps not the outside. I'll need a candle."

Angie handed her one.

"Ah..." Madame Hermione touched her forehead with her fingertips as she glided from the living room towards the master bedroom. "I feel something. A presence! Yes, there is certainly something 'other' in this house."

"She's the thing that's 'other'," Cat muttered. "This is already ridiculous and it hasn't even started yet!"

"This is about more than making another sale, Cat!" Maria insisted. "It's about Angie's happiness!"

Angie didn't want to hear their arguing and hurried after Hermione, wondering what she was up to. The bedroom was empty.

Connie pointed to the bathroom. Hermione was in there holding the candle high, looking at the ceiling, and turning in a circle. "Don't even ask," Connie whispered. Angie shrugged.

Hermione came out, briefly stepped into the den, looked at the stairs to the upstairs bedrooms, and turned away from them. Finally she fluttered, as much as a 300-pound woman can flutter, across the living room to the kitchen. "Nothing!" she cried. "Whoever lived here wasn't much of a cook."

Angie didn't follow her into the kitchen, but instead muttered, "I don't know if that's good news or bad."

"Madame Hermione is what's bad news," Cat said, disgusted. Angie had forgotten her sister had the hearing of a Doberman. "This is a joke. I thought better of Connie, frankly. Are you sure you don't want to just call it quits now, Angie?"

"Don't be silly. Connie went to a lot of trouble to arrange this séance, and we're going to see it through," Angie said as Hermione and Connie returned to the living room. She picked up the chardonnay bottle. "Connie? Madame Hermione?"

"Yes!" Connie said, holding out a glass for Angie to pour.

"I suggest not." Madame Hermione frowned at Connie and then everyone else with wine. "We need all our faculties for this event. Afterward, however, wine and perhaps some little nibblies would be most satisfying."

The only "little nibblies" Angie had brought were the nuts and pretzels already out, and Madame Hermione looked as if she could down an entire bowl in one gulp.

They gathered all the candles together, placed them in the center of the dining room table, and sat around it.

Madame Hermione ordered them to hold hands. She sat at one end of the table, Angie opposite her, with Maria and Cat on one side, and Connie on the other.

Hermione shut her eyes and began to hum what sounded like "Om," the chant Angie learned in a yoga class.

Hermione then spoke in a low voice. "I am calling to the spirit, or spirits, in this house. I feel your presence. Come to me! Reveal yourself!" She waited a minute, then repeated the words. A minute later she repeated them again.

Then she stopped and glared at the people sitting with her. "Someone isn't taking this seriously." Her dark eyes zeroed in on Cat, then flashed over to Angie. "I'm not sure who it is, but your negative vibes are bothering the spirits. They won't come where they aren't wanted or accepted."

"We'll try not to be negative," Angie said. She noticed Cat roll her eyes—all the sisters were eye-rollers. Angie had never realized how obnoxious the gesture could be. "Come on, everybody. I asked Connie to invite Madame Hermione here, as well as all of you, so the least you can do is cooperate."

Connie nodded; so did Maria. Cat glared.

Hermione repeated her invitation to the spirits. This time, she only said the words once, then stopped. "Yes, I feel you here! You're coming closer. It's all right. You're in the company of friends. Will you speak, spirit?"

They waited.

"*Spe-e-e-e-ak!*" Madame Hermione roared.

A squawky high "tweet" followed by a low "toot" came from the back yard.

"I'll be damned," Cat said. "It's the ghost of Benny Goodman."

"Speak to me, I command you!" Hermione ordered.

A noise like someone drumming on a garbage can struck next. Angie felt her heart beat quicken. It was weird, but scary.

"Give us a sign that you are here!" Hermione shouted, her voice loud but tremulous. "A sign! Any sign!"

They held their collective breaths, waiting.

"You need a better class of ghost, Angie," Cat muttered.

A light streaked across the ceiling. All five of them jumped.

"Ah! It's here! The ghost is here!" Hermione shouted. She changed her voice to one much higher and almost childlike. "Yes, ma'am, I am here."

"Who are you?" Hermione demanded. "Why are you here?"

Then she answered her own question in the little hushed voice. "I want to go home. Please set me free."

A low *toooot* sounded from outside.

"Oh? Ah!" Hermione cried. "We have more than one ghost. It's all right." She stood, still holding Connie's and Maria's hands. "I command you, be gone! Leave this house!"

The light, which Angie thought looked remarkably like a flashlight beaming in from the back yard, skittered over the ceiling a couple of times and then went out.

Hermione slowly lowered her hands and sat back down. "I will speak the words that I hope will rid the house of these spirits and keep them away." In a low voice she chanted, *"O vile sprit, o wraith, o spectre—"*

Something whimpered and scratched at the sliding glass door.

"It sounds like dog," Connie said. "But I can't quite see in the dark."

Angie took a candle and went to the sliding glass door to the back yard. A small white West Highland Terrier stood on its hind legs and rapped the glass with its front paws. "A little white Scottie dog," Angie said. "How cute. I wonder if he's hungry or thirsty."

She slid open the door to see if the dog was friendly or would just run away. To her surprise, he leaped into the house and ran past her straight to the kitchen. "Doggie, no!" She ran after him, trying to pick him up and get him back outside.

He darted from her and scurried to the pantry door where he began to whimper. She opened the door, but the pantry was quite bare. "I feel like Old Mother Hubbard," she said to the others who stood in the kitchen watching. "I wonder what this is all about."

"You might give him some water," Connie suggested. "He seems to know the house. Maybe he belongs to a neighbor."

Fortunately, the house still had some bowls, so she found one and filled it with water. The dog lapped it up as if dying of thirst. Then he ran over to a corner of the dining area, curled up, and shut his eyes.

"Look at that!" Angie cried. "He looks so sleepy. I say we leave him alone. It's cold and rainy outside, yet he somehow managed to stay dry. He's a pretty smart little dog, I'd say."

"Shall we attempt to continue?" Madame Hermione asked coldly. "I'm not sure, however, that I can bring back the proper ambiance, the proper—"

"Please try," Angie said.

They again sat at the table and held hands. Madame Hermione began swaying as she again chanted, "*O vile spirit, o wraith, o spectre—*"

A candle went out.

"Older houses can be drafty," Connie said quickly.

The others agreed, chuckling nervously, as Angie took a match and relit the candle.

A little louder, Hermione said, "*O vile—*"

As Angie blew out the match, another candle went out, then a second.

"What's going on?" Maria asked in a high, shaky voice.

"It's nothing. A draft, that's all," Cat said as Angie relit the candles.

A candle went out again; Angie relit it.

"So the house is drafty as well as haunted. It figures," Maria said. "Good job, Cat."

"The only windbag around here is you!" Cat snarled.

A different candle went out.

As Angie relit it, another one died.

Then another.

Cat yanked the matchbook out of Angie's hands and quickly relit all the candles. "That's how it's done!"

Hermione shouted. "*O vile spirit, o—*"

A candle flickered and then died.

"I don't feel any draft," Connie's voice trembled. "So why—"

"Obviously, the candle wicks are defective," Cat said, a little too loudly and a little too forcefully.

All the candles went out at once. The room plunged into darkness.

The dog let out a mournful howl; Angie's blood ran cold.

Maria jumped to her feet. "I'll find my purse. I've got a bottle of holy water."

A loud knock sounded on the door.

"My God!" Connie groaned, standing. "What's that?"

"Evil spirits!" Maria cried. "Don't let them in!"

"Ignore it!" Madame Hermione ordered as she, too stood up. "All of you! Sit back down right now! I can damned well do this in the dark! *Oooo viiiile spirit!—*"

But Angie knew that loud, no-nonsense policeman's knock. She stood, lit one candle and shielded the flame with her hand as she used it to light the way to the door and swung it open.

"What's going on, Angie?" Paavo asked as he strode inside wearing his grim inspector's face and dragging in with him a sopping wet, sheepish and scared Stan Bonnette holding a clarinet. Stan wore a slicker and rain hat, and Paavo's hand had a firm grasp on the slicker's back collar.

Paavo's gaze jumped from the Angie to the over-sized Madame Hermione, who stood and shouted strange words at the top of her lungs while flapping thick, gelatinous arms and ordering everyone to sit down.

Maria ran over and doused him and Stan with handfuls of holy water, then continued to splash it all around the room. Paavo let Stan go, and Stan scooted across the room faster than Angie had ever seen him move.

"Stan?" Angie gasped.

Paavo's eyes grew harder and more skeptical as they went from Maria to Cat who kept trying to light candles on the dining room table with little success, and Connie who awkwardly tried to help her.

"Connie, not you, too?" he said.

"This nonsense was all Connie's idea!" Cat cried, closing the book of matches and smacking them down on the table. "I'm leaving!" She grabbed her purse and jacket and hurried towards the door. "Lock up, will you, Angie?"

"Wait, Cat! Can you give me a ride?" Stan squeaked, then looked at Paavo. "That is...?"

"Go," Paavo said.

"Stan, what were you doing?" Angie asked.

He pointed at Connie. "It was all her idea!"

"It was not!" Connie yelled. "He was the one who worried about you, Angie. I only tried to help!"

Angie gave Stan a look that should have turned him to stone. He muttered incoherent goodbyes and keeping as far from Paavo as possible, darted out the front door after Cat.

"Who is this strange, unwanted fellow?" Madame Hermione demanded, pointing at Paavo. "And why has he caused such disruption to my séance?" Her eyes narrowed as she faced Connie. "I still expect to be paid, you know. It's not my fault I couldn't finish!"

"Paid for what? A sham?" Paavo asked stepping closer to her. He regarded Hermione without expression, but his question dropped the temperature in the room about ten degrees.

Connie jumped between the two, facing Paavo. "It's a party game, that's all," she babbled, then spun around to face Hermione. "Don't worry. I'll take care of it. He's Angie's fiancé, Inspector Paavo Smith, SFPD."

Hermione lifted her nose and regally sauntered towards the door. "Please drive me home."

"Gladly," Connie said as she grabbed her jacket and handbag.

Before leaving, Hermione looked back at Angie. "To you, this may have been a 'party game,' but there is a presence here. Most definitely."

"You don't have to pretend, Hermione," Connie said sheepishly. "The joke is over. There were no spirits—just you and Stan having fun. I'm sorry, Angie. I thought it was a good idea at the time. One that would make you think seriously about this house before buying it. You don't want to buy a place you have doubts about. But nothing turned out the way I planned. Again, I'm sorry."

"I'm not pretending," Hermione said. "Something is here...some presence. Let's get out of here, Connie." With that, head high, she marched out the door, Connie skulking at her heels.

"Angie, you idiot!" Maria shrieked, her holy water bottle empty now. "Don't you know that when you open the door to the occult and dark spirits, even if you're playing around, they just might take you up on it! Heaven help you!" With that, she stormed out as well.

As Maria pulled the door shut, Angie wished she could leave, too. Instead, she took a deep breath and faced Paavo. "You can clear out a party faster than anyone I've ever known." She gathered up the wine glasses and brought them into the kitchen. Paavo helped with those she couldn't carry, but after she put them down and turned to go back to the living room to get the cashews and pretzels she had put out, he caught her arm.

"Let's talk."

"Talk? About what?" she asked innocently. "And also, why are you here?"

"Bianca called and wondered what was going on. She told me about Cat and Maria arguing. She said she tried to find out more from Frannie, but she's not involved at all. It's clear Bianca can't handle her sisters knowing something that she doesn't. And she was worried. I had a good idea where I'd find all of you."

"Bianca needs to mind her own business! Cat never should have called her!"

"Bianca also said something about worrying about a person who chooses a friend over her own sister as her matron of honor." Paavo gave her a sidelong glance. "Is there another problem with the wedding plans?"

"There are always problems and hurt feelings with wedding plans! That's one of the things that makes them so emotional. Now, I've got to clean up everything before we leave." She again started towards the living room, when Paavo hauled her back.

"We aren't doing anything until we get this settled," he said. "I take it you honestly think this house is haunted."

"Of course not! I don't believe in ghosts! For pity's sake, Paavo! Do you think I'm crazy?"

"Crazy enough to put salt packets in your parents' house to ward off the evil eye," he said with a grin, remembering the story Serefina once told him.

"I was just a kid!" she insisted. "Besides, *all* Italians believe in the evil eye. It means nothing!"

"Calm down, and tell me why you were holding a

séance."

"It was because of Maria." She folded her arms. Paavo leaned back against the kitchen counter, one foot crossed over the other, as she explained how Maria wanted an exorcism but couldn't get one so Connie hired a friend who knows a bit about the occult to put on a show and then declare the spirits had left the premises. "We were doing it to convince Maria, who does believe in ghosts, that Madame Hermione managed to free them from this house. It was supposed to be nothing more than that. Although it seems Connie had other ideas and roped Stan in as well. Anyway, I simply tried to be a good sister, tried to get Maria to believe this house would be safe for her and my mother to come visit."

He wrinkled his mouth. "A good sister! I see."

The little white dog got up and padded to Angie. She could have kissed it, since it gave her an excuse to stop the interrogation. She handed it a plain pretzel, and he scarfed it down hungrily. "Poor baby!" she said as she gave it a couple more. "I wonder what we should do with him."

"Put water outside," Paavo said, squatting down to pat the dog's head. "He probably lives nearby. He's too well cared for to be a stray. I suspect he'll find his way back home. If he's still here tomorrow, Cat should contact the realtor in charge. They can decide if they want to try to find his owners or send him to the pound as a lost dog."

"He's much too cute for the pound! I hate to leave him."

He stood back up. "I'm sure he belongs to someone, Angie. He'll most likely go back home without the distraction of a bunch of people holding a séance. He probably came here to have a good laugh." At that, Angie watched his mouth slowly spread into a grin. "When I walked in," he said, "you can't imagine!" Paavo started with only a small chuckle, but soon he laughed hard.

Hands on hips, Angie shuddered at the memory of Maria smacking everyone with holy water, Cat and Connie furiously lighting candles that kept dying, the oversized seer bellowing for everyone to sit back down, and Stan looking like a newscaster reporting on a hurricane. When she opened the front door for Paavo, her sisters and Connie had gawked and cowered as if they expected someone to walk in with his head tucked underneath his arm.

Lifting her chin high, she announced, "I don't see what's in the least bit funny!"

Chapter 19

ON THE PHONE, Gillian from Wedding Vows had been the most unperturbed, placid person Angie had ever spoken with. Excited about meeting her face-to-face, she invited her to her apartment to talk, and now, a cherubic, fifty-something woman sat comfortably on her living room sofa.

"I want a traditional wedding—white dress, veil, five bridesmaids and bridegrooms, one flower girl—but I also want something unique and memorable," Angie said.

"That's a lovely idea." Gillian put on her reading glasses. "I brought my spreadsheet so you can see what we need to do and by when. Now, when is the wedding scheduled?"

"In four months, Saturday the 25th, at Sts. Peter and Paul's Church in North Beach."

"Four months? You said four months?" She looked over the top of her glasses. "Goodness gracious! And you're only now contacting me? Well, don't worry about it, we'll manage. That's why my spreadsheet is so valuable. Have you done anything at all, as yet?"

"Yes, quite a few things," Angie said. It seemed to her that four months was plenty of time.

"Let's go through this." Gillian slid her finger down her spread sheet as she read. "You'll need to decide on flowers for the reception and the church, corsages, boutonnieres, and whatever you want to give to the parents of the bride and groom. Next, the photographer. Do you want video or stills? Invitations—have you sent out invitations yet? I hope you've at least ordered decent looking ones already. The reception location—you must have that by now as well or it'll be a complete disaster! But if you haven't chosen a good place it'll be a disaster anyway. How will you get from the church to the reception, by the way? And how many people will you be responsible for moving? How will your guests get there? Have you chosen your rings yet? Tuxedos for the men? Bridesmaids dresses? Your dress? What about shoes? Your menu? The cake? Favors? Wine or hard liquor, or both? Champagne? And we can't forget music—music for the church, pre- and post-ceremony, a band for the reception. Do you want a cocktail hour? What about music for that? And we need to think about linens for the reception, and then there's—"

"Stop! You're making me so nervous, I can't stand it! I've done a lot of that, I think. Well, at least the menu and the cake. And I've booked the reception hall and church. But I haven't sent out invitations yet. And I haven't chosen my dress yet because...well, because. And I'm still trying to decide on the bridesmaids' dresses since they shouldn't clash with the style of my dress. And I haven't decided yet on the colors for them."

"Goodness gracious! That's as much as you've done? And the wedding in four months? No, no, noooo." Gillian brayed like a dying cow as she shook her head, all her previous placidity gone. "Such a disaster! All I can say is to do this right, we really should have twelve months.

Minimum. These things take time, and much careful thought." She took in a deep breath, and then announced, "You really must delay the wedding."

Angie was struck mute. When she found her voice again, she could scarcely contain her outrage. "Twelve months? I don't want to wait another year to get married! I've waited quite long enough already!" She felt her arms start to itch. Then the itchiness spread to her neck. Was she going to break out in hives on top of everything else?

"Well, it's up to you, of course," Gillian said. "If that's what you insist on, somehow, we'll manage. I'll collect a bunch of things from weddings I've put together and you can choose what you want. That'll help speed us up."

Had Angie heard her right? "You'll choose 'things' from other people's weddings?"

"That would be best," Gillian said firmly. "We can't have a disaster, now, can we? In fact, I'm thinking already of one especially nice wedding I planned. We worked on it for sixteen months! I can simply import what I did onto your spreadsheet, and that'll take care of most of the decision-making so we can concentrate on those items we have no choice but to change."

Angie stood, walked to her apartment door, opened it, and said, "Goodness gracious! I think it's time for you to leave."

Paavo tried his best not to think of the bizarre scene on Clover Street the night before, and instead to concentrate instead on why Wyndom and Bedford had been murdered. Was it, as Marilee suggested, a matter of mistaken identity that caused Gaia's death?

Listening to Angie talk about housing prices reminded him of something the twins' elderly aunt had said to him—

that they came into a lot of money when they sold their parents' home. Gaia's bank account and investments were substantial, but not for someone who sold a home in ritzy Kentfield. He wondered how much money she received and what had happened to it.

He looked for her financial papers and found she kept income tax forms and supporting documents going back to her early twenties. He had never seen anyone, not even accountants, with such neat and complete records. The sale of her parents' Kentfield home took place ten years earlier. After paying all costs, taxes, and dividing the money with her sister, she had grossed over a half a million dollars. Three months later, she wrote out a check to Thomas Greenburg for $300,000. He could find no evidence that she received anything in return for that money. So why had she given it to him?

He went back to the paperwork he'd collected on Greenburg, and found, as he remembered, a statement that an anonymous "angel" had given Greenburg $300,000 to start his business.

Now he knew the angel's name. But why had she done it?

Paavo headed to South San Francisco and Zygog Software.

A half hour later, he entered Thomas Greenburg's office.

Greenburg hunched over his computer, every bit as sloppily dressed and unwashed as the first time Paavo saw him.

Greenburg glanced up, but as soon as he saw the fierce scowl on Paavo's face his demeanor changed. He took his fingers off the keyboard and leaned back in his chair. "You're the cop who came here before."

"That's right."

"I told you, I didn't know the dead people. Why are you back?"

"At least I have your attention this time," Paavo said. "So you won't have any excuses."

"Excuses?" Greenburg's eyes darted from side to side, and he adjusted his glasses higher on his nose. "What do you mean?"

"Why did you say you didn't recognize Gaia Wyndom's photo?"

"Gaia Wyndom? I don't know. Maybe because I didn't."

"It's hard to believe you wouldn't recognize the person who was so important to you ten years ago."

Greenburg rubbed his chin. A few long whiskers showed it had been a while since he shaved. "People change in ten years. Anyway, I didn't deny she gave me start-up money."

"No, but you didn't offer it, either."

"Why should I? It doesn't mean anything. It has nothing to do with her death."

Paavo leaned on Greenburg's desk. "How do you know that?"

Greenburg scooted his chair back from the desk, but it bumped into the wall and he could go no further. "Why should it? That was a lifetime ago!"

"Why did she give you the money?"

"She was generous. And knew genius when she saw it."

"Sure she was. Now answer the question."

"How should I know?"

"Gaia Wyndom wasn't the type of person who gave away that kind of money for no reason."

Greenburg stood. "I don't like what you're saying to

me! I want to talk to my lawyer."

Paavo stepped directly in front of him. "In other words, you did something illegal. Something to do with hacking, I suppose."

Greenburg backed up until he reached the wall, then folded his arms and jutted out his bottom lip. "I'm not saying."

Paavo looked over the man and saw someone much more immature than his years warranted. He decided to back off. He walked over to a small table, pulled out a chair and sat, hands folded, and waited a moment before saying, "Look, Thomas. I really don't care about what you did ten years ago as a hacker as long as it didn't involve murder, treason, or something equally weighty." He paused and let his words sink in. "If you pulled some goofy stunt, I'm not going to waste my time doing anything about it. I simply want to get this murder solved. And I think you can help me."

Greenburg scrunched his lips. "How do I know I can I trust you?"

"Did you commit a major crime, such as murder?"

"No, not at all! Of course not! I'd never do that!"

"What then?"

He gave no response.

"Just between us," Paavo urged. "You have my word."

Greenburg put a finger in his ear and wriggled it around as he pondered what to do. After a while of this, he dropped his hand. "Promise?"

"Yes."

Greenburg bit his bottom lip a moment before speaking. "Just between us, Gaia told me she once had a twin sister, Urda Lee Wyndom. Urda died, and Gaia was constantly getting Urda's social security and other data mixed up with her own. She asked me to go into Federal and California records and remove all trace of Urda. I didn't think it was anything particularly wrong. After all, poor Urda was dead."

Paavo rarely heard a bigger bunch of B.S.. "You're saying she offered you $300,000 to do something you thought wasn't illegal or in any way wrong? You expect me to believe that?"

"Why shouldn't you? It's true. She was a nice woman. Honest. Just like me. If she had money to burn, so be it."

"How did Gaia find you to offer you this windfall?"

"I'm not naïve. I checked around. She read about me online, and tracked me down to offer me money. Actually, I thought that was pretty nice of her."

"What else did she say about Urda?"

"Nothing! I swear. Only that Urda had died."

"Why did you give her a job at Zygog?" Paavo asked.

"She said life bored her and she wanted to work."

"And?" Paavo asked.

Greenburg shrugged. "After a while of listening to her, I realized she wasn't as rich as I originally thought, and a whole lot crazier. I even considered that Urda might not be dead. Bottom line, I wanted to keep an eye on her. Anyway, it was just a job."

Paavo couldn't take any more of Greenburg. He got up and left the office.

Chapter 20

AFTER GETTING RID of her latest disastrous wedding planner, Angie pondered the prior evening's fiasco. She had had it with goofy ideas about the spirit world. Séances, Stan playing a demented Wizard of Oz hiding in the backyard, the whole nine yards. With friends like those...

Her phone rang. It was Connie, who said as she drove Hermione home, the seer insisted she felt a real presence in the house, even though she had never felt a presence anywhere before. Madame Hermione had Connie so scared, Connie believed her and now sided with Maria. Angie needed to forget about buying that house.

Angie hung up the phone without saying some very bad words.

When it rang again, she thought Connie might have come to her senses, but instead it was Cat. Cat informed her if she wanted that house she would have to find a new realtor because Maria threatened to kill or at least maim her if she didn't get Angie to walk away from the deal.

Angie hung up on her as well, wondering if you could divorce your family.

What was with these people sticking their noses into

her life? She, who was not in the least bit nosey and never got involved in other people's lives, didn't deserve such treatment!

She sat down to ponder what to do next.

She had learned a lot about Eric and Natalie Fleming's murder reading the *Chronicle*, but little about the two of them as people—little about what made them 'tick' so to speak.

If she understood them better, maybe then she could figure out why they died. Whether the two were "stuck" here as her mother suggested, or not, Angie wanted to know what had happened to them. Why had two young people with so much to live for had their lives taken away so horribly? She remembered their pictures, so alive, so vibrant. For them to have died that way was wrong, and terribly sad.

The two had died thirty years ago, but their friends and possibly others in their families were most likely still alive. For all she knew, they had brothers and sisters who could shed light on them. Even the former homicide inspectors on the case might be available to talk with, although the less she involved Paavo or Homicide, the happier she would be.

Angie was a woman on a mission as she went to City Hall and got copies of Natalie and Eric's death records. With the information on them, she went to genealogy programs on the internet and began to search for family members so she could talk to them and find out what, if anything, went on in Eric and Natalie's lives that might have made them a killer's target.

She knew that sometimes when tragedy first strikes, people are too shocked, too hurt, to think clearly. But the passage of time can help the mind make connections that were lost in the emotion of the moment.

Eric's parents, Benjamin and Irene Fleming, lived in San Rafael, just north of San Francisco. She telephoned and was surprised when Irene answered. She took a deep breath. No way could she tell a mother that some people suspected her son haunted his former abode. Instead, she came up with a story of being a journalist and writing a magazine article on unsolved murders in San Francisco, and wondered if the Flemings would talk to her.

Both were available at six o'clock that very evening.

Angie drove across the Golden Gate Bridge and arrived right on time.

"I'm surprised anyone is interested in Eric's death this many years later," Ben said. He and his wife were well into their 80's and still living in the same house as they did at the time of Eric's murder.

Angie was prepared for this. "I know that for many people, finding out why a tragedy happened and the person responsible helps bring closure. I'm hoping that you feel that way and would be willing to help me out."

Irene perched on the edge of the sofa. She found a Kleenex in her pocket and held it scrunched up in her hand. "I often thought my husband and I were the only people in the whole world who remembered Eric, or cared about what really happened to him. Many seem to believe he committed suicide. He would never do such a thing. Someone murdered him; he and Natalie both. I'm glad you're looking into the case. It might help."

"I hope so," Angie said. "I'm sure the police asked this question time and again, but can you tell me anything about him the days before his death? Was he happy with his wife? Did he ever say anyone scared him or threatened him?"

"He seemed happy and devoted to Natalie," Irene said. "And never seemed afraid of anyone."

"Irene?" Ben said as he looked at her long and hard. Finally, she gave a reluctant nod. "There was one thing we should mention," he said softly to Angie. "It didn't come out at the time because we didn't think it important and it would only cast a cloud over his life, but he had a lot of women around him. A lot of women. He was very good looking, and had money." Ben shrugged. "It was to be expected, I suppose."

"I see," Angie said, suddenly uncomfortable over the way this nice couple opened up to her. "And you think that might have contributed to his death?"

"Not really, but we thought someone who might be able to use the information should know about it."

"Thank you," she murmured, feeling even guiltier now. She decided to end this sham of a conversation. "Tell me, was Eric an only child?"

"No, we have a son who's one year older than Eric, and a daughter who's eight years younger."

"Would it be possible for me to talk with your son?"

"Certainly, but I have no idea what he could tell you that we can't."

Angie gently said, "I have four sisters, and I must admit that we don't tell our parents everything."

Irene wrote down her oldest son's name and address. "Here you go."

Bill Fleming, Eric's older brother, lived in Vacaville. Since Angie was already in the north bay, she asked Irene to phone and see if Bill was home and willing to speak to her. He was.

"Thank you for looking into this for us," Irene said to Angie after she hung up the phone. "I know Eric didn't kill his wife or himself. People who say that simply didn't know him."

"I believe he's innocent as well," Angie said. She was about to step out the door when a question came to mind. She nearly dismissed it, but then decided to ask. "I've read that Natalie had a dog who was very devoted to her. Do you know what kind of a dog it was?"

"Oh, yes," Irene said with a small smile. "I remember him. He was a sweet little thing. All the neighbors took care of him until he died of old age. His name was Jock. He was a West Highland Terrier, and white as snow."

Angie felt a cold chill ripple down her back as she walked out of the house.

Angie drove Highway 37 to Bill Fleming's home, arriving about an hour later. Bill didn't have his brother's good looks, or if he once had them, they had long dissolved into a mostly bald pate, large, round stomach, and weak eyes covered by thick tortoise shell glasses.

"Eric...he was the golden boy," Bill said. He and Angie sat in his living room. "Most of the time, people say, it's the eldest son that gets all the attention. In olden times, the eldest was the heir apparent, and younger sons didn't much matter. That wasn't the case at our house.

"Ironically, things only got worse after Eric died. From that point on, no one could ever live up to him. Sometimes I thought my parents wished I had been the one who died instead of Eric, but eventually I realized that wasn't the case. They put him on a pedestal precisely because he was dead. He couldn't disappoint them any longer, but remained frozen in time and was, to them, perfect."

"Wow, you sound as if he wasn't the ideal son they thought him to be," Angie said.

Bill's mouth crumpled with distaste. "Maybe I'm being too harsh, but I got pretty sick of him over the years. I didn't do so bad in my life! I've retired from a good job, I've got a wife, two kids, seven—"

"Maybe you can tell me more about Eric," Angie suggested. When she saw the hurt look on Bill's face, she knew what the problem was. No one was interested in him. And neither was she.

"Fine, then," he said angrily. "You want to know about Prince Eric, I'll tell you. He threw away his money, drank too much, did pot, even LSD for a time. After he started to make a lot of money on those stupid, nerdy, Silicon Valley start-ups, he turned to cocaine. That burned through his money like nobody's business."

"I see," Angie was shocked. She hadn't expected that. "Does that mean his marriage wasn't as perfect as everyone liked to say?"

Bill squeezed his eyes shut as if he was struggling with his answer, then he gave a shake of the head and looked at her. "He was a charmer, our Eric, but I think he really did love his wife. I can't see him shooting her. And definitely not shooting himself. Come to think of it, none of this is particularly helpful to you. He was clean by the time he died, I'm sure. Anyway, just thought I'd mention it."

"Thank you," she said. "There's one other thing I wonder about. Your brother and his wife were both wealthy, so I'm surprised to learn he lived in a rental. Do you have any idea what was going on there?"

"That's easy. They bought some land near Carmel, on the water, and were having a home built. It was going to be a beautiful place, over 5000 square feet. They died before it was finished."

"How terrible," Angie said. Somehow, the thought of

newlyweds trying to find a place to live, touched something deep inside her.

"Yes, it was. Eric liked cars and women. Not until he met Natalie did he settle down. He wasn't a bad person, just wild when he was young and single. I can say that now; now that over thirty years have passed."

"Thank you," Angie said, and gladly left the bitterness of that house.

Back in Homicide, Paavo told Yosh all he'd found out from Greenburg.

"There's something about these twins," Paavo murmured, as he studied both pictures on the murder board. "I don't know what it is, but they bother me."

"I know one thing," Yosh said, "paying someone $300,000 to obliterate your twin's name from government records shows a degree of hatred that's stunning."

"At the same time, the two obviously spent time together," Paavo said. "Gaia even cut her hair to look like her sister's."

"Weird. And we've found no close friends, and no social activities beyond the one person she apparently loved. Who lives like that?"

Paavo grimaced. It was hitting more than a little close to home. "She supposedly had a couple of cats, but I saw no sign of them," Paavo said. The irony that he, too, had a cat wasn't lost on him.

"I think I did see a payment to a veterinarian on one of her credit card bills," Yosh said. "I could find it and check if she had cats, and if so, what happened to them—although I don't know that it would matter to the case."

"If they were healthy and with her, where are they now? We should find out," Paavo said, as he focused on the case again. "Although her co-workers seemed to scarcely know her, all remarked at how upset she was, starting a few weeks ago. We need to figure out what happened then."

"The bartender that Bedford confided in said the same thing. Two weeks earlier, Bedford was upset," Yosh said.

"We've got to find out—"

"Tomorrow!" Yosh insisted, standing up and putting on his jacket. "Let's call it a day."

"Sounds good," Paavo said, grabbing his jacket as well. "Say, are you free tonight, by any chance?"

"What, is Angie giving you some time off?" Yosh asked with a chuckle.

"Something like that," Paavo said.

"Lucky you. I've got to get home. The wife will remove my thick head from the rest of my very ample body if I don't go with her to a parent-teacher conference tonight for our youngest. He's a good kid, but he likes to act up in class, and the wife's worried about how bad the teacher's report will be."

So much for social activities, Paavo thought. "Good luck tonight!"

As Yosh walked away, Paavo felt a cold chill down his back. Would he have to face teachers talking about his kids some day? He couldn't imagine being a father. Maybe that was because he'd never known one. He knew nothing about trying to raise a kid, or what a father should be like. He'd probably only disappoint Angie in that, just the way he disappointed her with her wedding plans.

His father figure was Aulis, who was already a fairly old man when Paavo and his sister Jessica moved in with him. Aulis gave him love and support, especially after Jessica died. But Aulis didn't have a clue what Paavo did when he was a teenager, or the types of kids he ran around with. His life could have turned out a whole lot different than it had if he hadn't joined the army. That's what saved him.

Saved him?

Sometimes he wondered. If he had kept running with the gangs he'd gotten mixed up with in high school, at least he'd have friends. At least he'd have a best man.

Now, he had no one but co-workers...and Angie.

At times like this he wondered, was it enough?

Chapter 21

A NGIE SAT ALONE at a table by the front window of Wings of an Angel, the restaurant owned by three ex-cons who had become friends, Vinnie Freiman, Bruce Pagozzi, and Earl White. She went there for lunch, a plate of spaghetti in front of her, but she morosely picked at it.

"How you doin', Angie?" Vinnie said. He was short, stocky, in his sixties, and generally considered the brains of the operation.

"Not so good," she said.

He nodded. "Yeah, Earl said you was lookin' kinda glum. Anything you wanna talk about? Ol' Vinnie's here for you, you know?"

"I know, Vinnie. I appreciate it. Have a seat, please." She gestured towards the empty chair at her table. He sat. "My friends think I'm crazy, and they may be right."

"Miss Angie, we all know you always been a little wacky, but since when's that a problem? What's goin' on?" He picked up a piece of French bread from the basket, tore off a morsel and plopped it in his mouth.

"I found a house, a beautiful house, in the Sea Cliff part of the city. Paavo likes it, I love it, we can afford it. But there's something odd in its past, and now Connie and

Maria think the place is haunted!"

"Come on, now, Miss Angie, you don't believe in no ghosts. What do the people say who's livin' in it now? Are they afraid of these ghosts?"

"Nobody lives in it. No one has for thirty years." She took a sip of her pinot noir. "The owner wouldn't sell, and now her daughter is trying to sell it."

"The owner's dead, is she? Is she the ghost?"

"I don't think she is dead, just old. And she's not the ghost. Everyone suspects the ghosts are tenants who died near the house in a murder-suicide over thirty years ago."

"Forget the tenants, they's done for," Vinnie said. "You gotta focus on the living. Every time I think I saw a ghost, it was somebody playin' tricks, somebody who wanted to scare the crap outta me. Pardon my French. Why didn't the owner wanna sell the place if no one was livin' there? You gotta be nuts to sit on land that's a gold mine. That ain't makin' no sense."

"Oh, my God, you're right! You're a genius!" Angie stood, leaned across the table and kissed him. "I've been concentrating on the wrong people! Somebody wanted that house to stay empty, and kept it empty for thirty years! I'll bet whoever it was, still wants no one to live there!"

Vinnie blushed from head to toe at her kiss, a big smile on his face. "You keep us posted on this house business, Miss Angie," Vinnie said. "And now, what's happenin' with your weddin' plans?"

Angie was sure Vinnie meant well asking about her wedding, but that, too, wasn't the happiest of subjects for her, although not half as unhappy as ghosts. She soon finished her lunch, and left Wings of an Angel in a much better frame of mind than when she entered. Her three friends always had that effect on her, and she loved them dearly.

Time to scour the internet once more, she thought. How had anyone survived without it?

As she drove, Angie mentally went through the information she already had. Both Flemings were shot to death. Their house showed no break in, which meant they most likely knew their murderer.

The case was considered a murder-suicide only because Eric was found holding a gun and there were no viable suspects. The gunpowder residue proved inconclusive.

The police learned that the Flemings liked to throw parties, which meant many people's DNA would have been all over the house. Paavo hadn't mentioned to her anything about DNA tests, or if they were even available back then. He did say that the police conducted many interviews with people who knew the couple or had worked with Eric, but they could find no motive.

A car honked at her. In the rearview mirror, Angie saw a matronly driver indicating that Angie was "number one."

When had that light turned green?

She drove on. Basically, all speculation was based on fact that no one had any reason to kill the couple, and fell back on domestic violence as the reason for their deaths.

Yet, those same conclusions may have stopped the police from pursuing other motives and suspects.

She stomped on the brakes just in time as someone turned left in front of her. She was again number one! It wasn't her fault...at least, she didn't think it was. Being much more careful, she finally reached home.

She had already learned that the owner of the property at 51 Clover Lane was named Carol Steed, and that she had also been owner of the property when Eric and Natalie lived there.

Angie decided to find out more about Carol Steed and anyone else who knew the Flemings.

She then investigated the name of the owner across the street at 60 Clover Lane. She suspected whoever lived there at the time of the murders might have information for her. She was shocked to learn that Carol Steed also owned that property.

Puzzled by this, she spent quite a bit of time searching San Francisco birth, death, and marriage records on the Steed family. Eventually a picture emerged.

Carol Steed was born Carol Ramsey in 1938. She married Edward Steed in 1965. They had one daughter, Enid, born in April 1979. In October 1978, however, before Enid's birth, Edward Steed died in a fall.

As Angie previously learned, the two Clover Lane homes were built in 1950 by Edward's parents, Donald and Mary Steed, and after Mary's death, Edward became owner of both houses.

She now discovered that he and Carol had been living in the smaller of the two homes, and then moved into the big Clover Lane house when it became vacant.

Angie then went back to the notes Paavo had given her from the crime scene report. Eric Fleming had moved into the big 51 Clover Street house in November, 1978, one month after Edward's death. That must have meant Carol moved back into the smaller house. But why did she give up the bigger, more beautiful home?

Angie considered that Carol might have had only a small income, and rented out the bigger house so that she could have enough money to live on. But if she needed money, she would have rented the house out again after the Flemings were killed. No one would have moved into it immediately after the murders, but a year or two later, few people would have remembered. So money couldn't have been the reason she gave Eric the big house to rent.

Suddenly, all Angie's instincts went on red alert.

First, she went back to the marriage records and looked up Eric and Natalie. Their wedding took place in November 1979. Eight months later, both were dead.

She then got into her car and drove back to the *Chronicle*, and hurried back to its morgue to see if she could find anything about Edward Steed's death, since he supposedly died in an accident of some sort.

She found an article written one day after he died. Edward Steed had been scrambling on the cliff above China Beach and slipped on the rocks. Reports were that he must have hit his head on a rock or boulder as he fell because one side of his head, near the temple, had been struck hard enough to kill him.

Angie knew a person could die in a fall along some sections of the cliff over China Beach, but for the most part, the way the hill sloped, the fall would be more painful and "scrape-inducing" than a break-your-neck kind of drop unless a person was truly unlucky.

The report quoted Carol Steed as saying her husband climbed on the cliffs for fun because it was a beautiful, sunny October day, and he slipped.

Angie did a quick calculation...Carol's daughter Enid was born in April, so the prior October when Edward died, Carol would have been only a couple of months pregnant— far enough along that she would know—but not so far that the pregnancy would show. Carol was 41 when Enid was born. She and Edward had been married for thirteen years with no children when Carol found herself pregnant.

The very next month Carol moved out of the big house

and let Eric Fleming move into it. He was 28 years old at the time, handsome, single...and if his parents were correct, a womanizer, and according to his brother, enjoyed drugs and alcohol.

So, Angie thought, what if Eric met a lonely wife who lived in a beautiful home, got her pregnant...and *poof!* the husband was suddenly out of the picture?

Angie had her suspicions about what had happened, but how could she prove any of it?

Why in the world didn't the police investigators at the time have the kind of mind she did?

Maybe because they were there; they saw Natalie and knew about her money and beauty. They also saw the landlady. For all Angie knew, she was gorgeous, but if so, the police might have suspected something. Most likely, she wasn't much to look at, a dozen years older than Eric, and that was why thoughts of anything going on between Eric and his landlady never even crossed their minds.

She went back to the online genealogical program she had used earlier to find Eric Fleming's relatives. In it, she learned that Carol Steed's daughter's married name was Enid Norbel and she still lived in San Francisco.

She then phoned her sister, Cat. "The person who wants to sell the Clover Lane house, the owner's daughter, is named Enid Norbel, right?"

Cat didn't answer right away. "How do you know that?"

Angie smiled. *"Ve haf our vays!* Thank you!"

She quickly hung up. She didn't want Cat quizzing her, and she didn't want to lie to her sister.

Chapter 22

ANGIE TORE HERSELF away from her discoveries and dashed across town for an appointment. She was both glad and surprised to find a nervous Paavo already there.

She led him to the office area of St. Peter and Paul's church. They were there to talk to the priest about being married in the church.

"Father John, this is my fiancé, Paavo Smith," Angie said as she introduced the two men. "Paavo, Father John."

"Hello, Father," Paavo said shaking hands with the priest. Father John was in his forties, of medium height and build, with short graying hair that was quite thin on top.

"I know Angie and her family well," Father John said, "although I don't see her as often as I should."

"I know; I'm sorry," Angie murmured. She had warned Paavo that Father John was an old enough priest to enjoy inflicting a little old-fashioned Catholic guilt on his parishioners. Paavo would have preferred a new-style, anything-goes priest, but he knew that wasn't Angie's way or her family's.

The priest turned to Paavo. "Paavo—that's a Finnish name, isn't it? Are you Finnish?"

"My father was," he said. "He died. My guardian was also Finnish."

"I suspect you were raised Lutheran," Father John said with a smile. "Most Finns are."

"I've been told I was baptized in a Lutheran Church, and when I was young I went to a Lutheran church with my step-father," Paavo said. "But once away from my guardian, I pretty much stopped going."

"A common situation with many young people these days, I'm afraid. Tell me, do you still consider yourself a Christian?" Father John asked.

Paavo moved uncomfortably in his seat. "As much as I have any religious belief, it is the Christian way of thinking that I most follow."

"What about children? Would you want them to be raised as Catholics?"

"I would raise children as Catholic, and I would attend church with them and Angie." He looked at her. "I would like to do that."

Father John nodded and then studied the couple a long moment. "I'm sure there will be no problem with the two of you getting married in the church. We'll be glad to have you here. Who knows, someday you might decide to join us and become a convert."

"Angie can be persuasive," Paavo said.

"I know the Amalfi women. And you're right," the priest said with a chuckle. Angie had convinced the priest to let her break the news to Paavo that they would also be attending the church's pre-marital classes.

Father John ended the visit with a few words about the sanctity of marriage and the life-long commitment the two were entering with each other. He then gave a brief prayer for their future happiness, and made a sign of the cross with Angie. He placed his hand on Paavo's shoulder as he made a sign of the cross over him, praying that one day he would find solace in his marriage, and in his life.

Paavo found himself surprisingly shaken by the encounter. How had the priest known he had no solace in his life? Was it that obvious? He felt as if he had been on a hot seat in there. He was so used to the modern way of looking at marriage and divorce, and how easily people moved from one state to the other, that he forgot that in a great part of the world marriage wasn't a whim of the moment. And to Angie and church-going Catholics, it was a sacrament. He didn't know much about the Catholic church, but he knew that there were only seven sacraments, so it was a big deal.

He was glad to leave, but at the same time, both the priest's blessing and his words about the sanctity and seriousness of what they were about to undertake had moved him deeply.

After meeting with the priest, Paavo was more than happy to go with Angie to dinner at the Russian Renaissance Restaurant. He immediately ordered vodka. He rarely touched hard liquor and it rather amused and moved Angie to see the effect meeting the priest and talking about their marriage had had on him. Maybe he wasn't as immune to religion as he thought.

By the time their dinner of borsch, stroganoff, and potato vareniki was delivered, the conversation turned to Paavo's intertwined cases.

"I've got two people who worked together," he said. "The man, Taylor, was married and having an affair with the identical twin sister of Gaia, the woman who was killed."

"The obvious question is how jealous was Taylor's wife?" Angie asked.

"She doesn't seem jealous at all. I have the impression the two lived together but didn't much like each other. The wife is beautiful, movie star good looks."

"Did the wife know Gaia had an identical twin?"

"I doubt it. Few people knew, not even her co-workers. To hear them, she had no one in her life, no friends, relatives, had never been in love, and so on. Also, she and her twin didn't get along. Most people said they thought Gaia lived for TV shows and her cats. Period. She had no interest in the news, politics, movies, or music."

"So she basically had nothing going on in her life, and then she was murdered?" Angie asked.

"One other thing, Taylor's secretary, an older man, gave every indication that Taylor might have had a tryst or two with him as well."

"Really? The wife had to suspect something was wrong with her marriage, or she's an idiot. Women know, even if they don't want to admit to anyone."

"You think so?" he asked.

"Absolutely. She knew he was a cheat, and finally decided to do something about it. The beautiful wife probably found out that her husband had thrown her over for those two and felt so insulted that she killed him. I suspect she didn't realize the woman who worked in his office was the wrong sister. Poor Gaia!"

"It doesn't quite ring true," Paavo said. "If she murdered them, she had to have paid someone to do it since Taylor was stabbed to death with a powerful thrust I doubt she could had inflicted. Gaia was killed after Taylor—or so we assume because she called her boss to say she was sick and couldn't come in to work. Now that I think about it, though, it could easily have been Marilee who phoned the office, pretending to be Gaia."

Thoughts swirled in his mind.

"The medical examiner is still trying to determine the time and date of Gaia's death in the face of some strange findings. Usually, when people are killed because of a jealous rage, both are killed at the same time—and the most likely place would have been their beach cabin."

"Except that would have pointed straight at the wife," Angie said. "And everyone would know Taylor had been cheating on her. The wife wouldn't want that."

"Good point, Angie. I knew I kept you around for some reason."

"Something more is out there. Some missing piece. Once you find what it is, it'll all fall together," she said, then added. "The same thing is going on with my murder case."

"*Your* murder case?"

"The Flemings." She smugly nodded, leaned closer and lowered her voice. "It was no murder-suicide. Someone killed them both. But I don't yet know why. I've got an idea, though. I'm looking at the landlady."

"The landlady? That's a pretty harsh penalty for being late with the rent."

"Very funny! I think she might have been in love with Eric Fleming."

Just then, Paavo's phone began to vibrate. He normally would have shut it off, but he saw the call was from Katie Kowalski. "I better take this."

He got up and stepped into the hallway that led to the restrooms, away from the diners. "Hello."

"Uncle Paavo?" the young voice asked.

"Micky, how nice to hear you," Paavo said, worried

that the child would be phoning him. "Is everything all right?"

"Yes. I wanted to tell you I'm on the Panthers T-ball team now," Micky said. "I hit every ball!"

"Hey, great job! I'm proud of you!"

"I wish you could have seen me," Micky said softly.

Something about the way he said it, made Paavo's heart catch. "I do, too, Micky. But your Mom was there, wasn't she?"

"Yes."

"And her new friend?" Paavo asked.

Angie stood in front of him now. She'd been watching his face and knew something was wrong.

"What friend?" Micky asked.

Paavo wasn't sure what to say, but Katie had told him... "Maybe I misunderstood," he began carefully. "I thought your Mom had a friend, a man named Daniel or Dan, who liked to watch you play ball."

"No. She comes by herself. She looked a little sad. I think she wished you were there, too."

Paavo shut his eyes a moment. "When is your next game, Mick?"

"Tuesday, five o'clock, at Funston."

"I don't know for sure if I can be there, okay? I can't make promises because of my job. You understand that, right Micky?"

"Yes. But will you try?"

"I'll try."

"Good. I miss you, Uncle Paavo."

"I miss you, too, son. I'll see you soon, okay?"

"Okay."

"Bye, now."

Paavo hung up and looked at Angie. "There's no man

in Katie's life according to Micky."

Angie nodded. "And there won't be as long as you're there as someone for her to lean on and to keep the past alive. You understand that, don't you?"

"I do. But Micky doesn't. It's hard on the boy."

"On you, too," she said, and put her arm around his waist. He didn't have many people in his life that he loved. Micky was one of them, and now he'd been asked to stay away. No words would help, and this was a situation with which she dare not interfere.

Chapter 23

ANGIE RANG THE doorbell at Enid Norbel's house. A tall, attractive woman with brown hair and eyes opened the door. "I'm looking for Enid Norbel. My name is Angelina Amalfi, and—"

"Oh, yes." Enid immediately warmed up to the visit. "You're the person who keeps going to see my house! I hope you aren't here to negotiate on the price."

"No, not at all—"

"But you still like it?" Enid asked.

"Definitely," Angie said. "Very much. I'm sorry to bother you, and I know this isn't the way things are usually done, but I'd like to talk to you about it, if I may?"

"Certainly. Come on in." As they walked to the living room, Enid said, "A friend recommended that I offer whichever realtor sold the house a $20,000 bonus over and above any commissions they might receive. I told your sister that when she called, and that's all I'll say on that score!"

"I'm not here to talk money," Angie said. She now understood Cat's sudden interest in selling the place, and her generosity in turning over the commission as a wedding present!

Angie sat on the sofa, and Enid on the love seat facing her. "My grandfather built the house," Enid said. "What did you want to know about it?"

"Did you ever live there?"

"No. My mother moved to the smaller house across the street after my father died, before I was born."

"I assume she rented out the big house because she could get more money from it than from the little place," Angie said.

"Not really. My father left her well off. She never said why she moved. The small house was roomy enough for the two of us. I assumed the bigger house reminded her of my father. She was desperately in love with him, and never got over his death."

"I see. That would make sense," Angie said.

"To tell the truth, I think she both loved and hated the 51 Clover Lane house. My father died while they lived there, and later, some tenants who were living there also died—not in the house, of course. A murder-suicide, apparently. My mom said the ordeal was a nightmare with the police and newsmen tramping all over and asking everyone questions. I think she decided she didn't want to bother with any more tenants. Oh, dear! Perhaps I shouldn't be saying all this. It might make the house seem undesirable to you. But no one died in the house. Not even all that close to it!"

"No, it's all right," Angie said. "I already knew about all that."

"Good." Enid sounded relieved. "Actually, my mom often said that if she found someone she could love, she would want to live in the big house with him, so she never held anything against the house as you can see! Unfortunately for her, she never fell in love again. Now it's too late."

Angie found this conversation terribly sad. "Too late? Is she sick?"

Enid fidgeted. "Well, if you buy the house, it'll come out so I may as well explain now. My mother has a mental illness. It's not something easy to put a name to. She's borderline paranoid schizophrenic. Not dangerous since her medication stabilizes her, but she tends to live in her own little world that has nothing to do with reality. It's easy to hold a conversation with her on the simplest level. 'What would you like for dinner?' 'Do you want to watch television?' But if you try to talk to her about anything complex, she can't follow it. People say she had some sort of a nervous breakdown after my father died. She was always troubled, and she's gotten worse over the years. Recently, I was granted conservatorship over her finances."

"I'm so sorry about your mother," Angie said. "Does she live with you?"

"She spends most days at a care facility, Restful Gardens in the Richmond district. It's nice, but terribly expensive. That's why I'd like to sell 51 Clover Lane. Unlike my mother, I have no reason to keep it."

"I see."

"On good days, they allow her to go home, which is nice for her."

"Home? To 60 Clover?"

"Yes. When she's there, a nurse's aide stays overnight with her. But I doubt she'll be able to go home much longer. I haven't decided yet, when that time comes, if I want to sell that house as well, or simply rent it. It's not as special as 51 Clover, but still a beautiful piece of property."

"Yes, it is," Angie said, then after a slight pause, asked, "I'm wondering if it would be possible for me to speak to your mother?"

"She doesn't talk to strangers. She's easily frightened."

"You think she'd be scared of me?"

"When she sees someone she doesn't know, she often thinks the person is a ghost."

Angie was taken aback. "She thinks she sees ghosts?"

"Yes, it's crazy."

"Was she institutionalized because she thinks she sees ghosts?" Angie asked.

"She not only sees them, but she believes they're after her and want to kill her."

Angie's left eye began to twitch. "I see. Um...did she ever say who haunted her?"

"Not directly," Enid answered. "But from things she said, I think she believes she's being haunted by her renter, the woman who was murdered. Oops...maybe I shouldn't have said that. But you did say you know about the renters."

"Yes, Natalie and Eric Fleming."

"My goodness, you have done your homework, haven't you? I scarcely remembered their names myself! But she once said a little thing that made me think she referred to the dead woman."

"What was that?"

Enid smiled. "You'll probably laugh, and I guess it is funny. Like I said it was a little thing, but I remember it clearly. She said that before the ghost showed up, she knew she was coming because 'she smelled Joy'. Not until years later did I learned Joy was the name of a perfume!"

Angie felt a cold chill. "Yes, my mother used to wear it as well. It's a beautiful, expensive and memorable scent."

"Well, there you go! Maybe you are meant to buy the house," Enid said with a chuckle. "Especially if the ghost shows up and you like her taste in perfume. Anyway, I never considered a perfume-wearing ghost to be anything that I or anyone else should be afraid of."

"Did you ever consider that your mother might have been right—that the house is haunted?"

Enid laughed. "Of course not! If I had, I'm sure I'd have been sent to a loony bin like my mom." She then grew much more serious. "I'm sorry to say that my mother spent her life grieving for my father. Unfortunately, while grieving for him, she forgot that she had a daughter who was very much alive. She gave me next to no attention as I grew up, and now that I'm an adult with my own family, I do what I must with her. No more, no less."

"I can't say that I blame you for that," Angie said, her expression sympathetic. She guessed she had been completely wrong about the landlady being in love with Eric if she grieved that desperately for her husband.

But, while Angie could understand the portrait Enid had painted of Carol's grief, she also saw how unfair it was to the child.

Seeing Angie's empathy, Enid continued, "I must admit she never seemed all that crazy to me, but once she started talking about ghosts, well, I couldn't argue against sending her away."

Angie swallowed hard. "I guess not. Can you tell me...when did she start having these hallucinations and other problems?"

"As long as I can remember, actually. As I say, she never got over my father's death. She mourned him every day and said he was the love of her life. She often said she wished she had died when he did, which would have meant I was never born. I don't think she even considered that. I'll tell you, it was a pretty devastating thing for a child to hear."

"I can imagine. How terrible for you, and tragic for her."

"She had no family, and neither did father. It's hard to believe these days, but I don't even have any pictures of him except one. She said she burned them all after he died because she was so angry with him for 'getting himself killed by being stupid' as she put it."

"Surely, she didn't destroy her wedding pictures," Angie said, knowing what a huge part of wedding planning the photo shoots would be.

"She and my father eloped, so there weren't any special wedding photos. Keep in mind that well before any doctor diagnosed her, my mother was 'not quite right' in the head. She kept one photo of my father, and she didn't show it to me until years later. I have to say, he was every bit as handsome as she claimed him to be. If you're interested, I'll show you."

"Well...sure," Angie said. She wasn't particularly interested, but remembering Bill Fleming's angry reaction when she implied she didn't care to hear about him, she didn't want to insult Enid.

Enid went into another room and soon came out with a framed photo and handed it to Angie.

Angie tried to keep her expression bland as she stared at the photo. Smiling back at her was Eric Fleming. Angie looked more carefully at Enid now. Her early suspicions about Carol Steed's relationship with her tenant—at least while he was single—as well as the reason Carol suddenly found herself pregnant after thirteen years of marriage, were confirmed. Clearly, Enid had never seen Eric Fleming's photo, and Angie wasn't about to be the one to tell her. "So this is your father, Edward Steed?" Angie asked.

"That's right," Enid said.

"He was very handsome," she said, handing the photo back. "And I do see the family resemblance. Thank you for showing me."

"It's all I have of him," Enid said, running her finger along the edge of the frame to remove dust. "People who have families are very lucky. That's why my husband and I have four children. They're grown up now, and are starting to have children of their own. We have three grandchildren so far and hope for many more. It's a blessing to me. I often think if my mother weren't so alone, she wouldn't have had these mental problems. Now, she can't even enjoy the family she has."

"I'm sorry, too," Angie said. "If you don't object, I really would like try to speak to her one day soon. If I frighten her, I'll quickly leave."

"Well, I won't say no, although I doubt it'll work out for you. I'll give you a signed note so the care home will allow you in. I hope you won't be too disappointed by how little she'll be able to tell you."

"Me, too."

After writing the note, Enid walked Angie out to her car. "I also hope all this background information hasn't soured you on the house," Enid said. "It's a lovely place, and deserves a happy, loving family in it. I think you may be just what it needs."

"Thank you," Angie said as she got into the car. She had a lot to think about.

Paavo found an old receipt for a prescription of sleeping pills among Gaia's financial papers, which made it likely she had taken the pills herself. The case looked more and more like suicide except for one problem—why?

Back in Homicide, Paavo noticed that a cancelled check for $350.00 had just been posted to Gaia's checking account. Apparently, no word had reached the bank that the account should have been closed.

He got a copy of the check and saw it had been made out to Brian Riddingham on the Tuesday before Taylor Bedford died. Gaia almost never wrote out any checks.

Paavo looked into Riddingham. Only one person with that name lived in San Francisco.

A half-hour later he stood at Riddingham's door, asking about the check.

He learned that Brian and his wife had sold a white Kenmore freezer to Gaia Wyndom. They hadn't cashed her check right away, and never realized she wasn't still alive.

They had been curious as to why Gaia wanted the freezer—usually a single woman living alone doesn't want or need a large chest-type freezer. She wouldn't say, paid the asking price, and hired someone who picked it up the very afternoon of the sale.

Riddingham knew nothing more.

No freezer had been found in Gaia's house, and no clue as to what had happened to it.

Paavo went to see Evelyn Ramirez, the Medical Examiner. "You were talking about time of death and strange findings on the body temperature. You said it might have been because the body had been in bathwater for some time before being found. What if there's another reason? What if the body was frozen after death and then put in the bathtub to defrost?"

"Sort of like quickly defrosting a turkey in water before Thanksgiving?" The M.E. said with a smirk, but then she gave it some thought. "You know, that could be it! That would make sense. But to freeze a human body? That would take—"

"A large, chest-style freezer?"

"Exactly."

Paavo's next job was to find the freezer.

He began phoning haulers and charitable organizations to see if any had pick-ups from Gaia Wyndom's home. Hours later, he hit pay dirt: she had called a junk hauler to pick up a freezer and bring it to the dump. She had made the call on a Tuesday, one week after buying the freezer, and one day after she called in sick at work.

Paavo met the truck driver and found the freezer relatively easily. He had it delivered to the CSU so the crime scene investigators could go over it with a fine-tooth comb.

They found some hairs that matched Gaia's, which made sense since it was her freezer, but nothing else.

Angie told herself she only chose to return to the house to check on the little dog.

When she got there, she couldn't find him. She hoped Paavo was right about him living in the neighborhood, and he had found his way home.

Once in the house, however, she again had the sense of being welcomed, that this could be home for her and Paavo, a happy home.

"All right. I can't take this anymore," she said to the walls. "Eric? Natalie? Are you here?" She suddenly had visions of herself as Cosmo Topper dealing with the ghosts of George and Marian Kirby. She had watched the old black and white film as well as the old TV shows many times as a child with her mother. She had found them hilarious back then. Now, not so much.

"If there's something here I should worry about, I want to know it. I don't want to start out in a house with Paavo that is going to cause us grief. I need to know right now, immediately!"

Nothing happened.

Feeling increasingly foolish, she sat down on the sofa, waiting, but soon got up and went to the refrigerator. She had left an unopened bottle of Chardonnay in it the night of the séance. Sitting around waiting for ghosts to appear was definitely a reason for some wine.

To her surprise, the wine was gone. She looked in the trash receptacle under the sink and found the empty bottle there.

Who would have come in here and drunk her wine? That meant she wasn't the only person interested in the house. But to drink a whole bottle? That seemed a bit rude!

She opened the dishwasher. Inside were two stemmed glasses. She had washed, dried and put away the few glasses and dishes used for her séance 'party' the night before. What were these doing here? And why two of them?

"Eric? Natalie?" Her voice quavered.

Just then, she heard what sounded like the glass door in the living room sliding on its track, and then the 'thud' when it shut against the door frame. Had someone just entered the house? She froze, scared.

It couldn't have been a ghost, could it? They didn't need to open doors to enter a room, did they? She quietly slid open a drawer to look for a knife for protection, but it held nothing more lethal than a butter knife. She took one out of desperation.

Holding it with two hands, she peeked into the living room.

It was empty.

Cautiously, she eased her way to the glass door. It was unlocked. She snapped the lock into place. Had someone been inside the house when she entered, and snuck out when they heard her go into the kitchen?

If so, she wasn't about to stick around to find out. Faster than she thought possible, she ran out of the house to her car, locking the doors as soon as she got in. The little dog must have found its way home, and so would she.

Chapter 24

CAT ARRIVED AT Angie's home at 10 a.m., surprisingly early, since Cat usually didn't face the light of day until 9 a.m., and took another two hours to dress, fix her hair, and put on make-up.

Last evening, Angie had phoned her and told her someone had been inside the Clover Lane house and left through the back door, leaving it unlocked. Cat then knew Angie had duplicated the house key and proceeded to lecture her about it. Angie assumed she was now here to demand the key.

"Have you chosen a wedding planner yet?" Cat asked as she sauntered into the living room.

Her words were a surprise. But if Cat wanted to make Angie feel bad, she had succeeded. "No," Angie confessed. "I just don't know what to do! I'm spending more time trying to find someone to hire than I am working on my wedding plans."

"What about your dress?" Cat asked.

"No."

"Bridesmaids' dresses?"

"No!"

"Wedding party?"

"*No!*" Angie grew more frantic with each question.

"All right, calm down. We're going to do it this way. I'll take charge of the clothes for everyone. Bianca, who's the 'people person,' will handle the guest list, reservations, and dealing with caterers and so on; Maria and her husband will handle the music at the church and the reception, plus the photographer; Frannie will be in charge of decorating the church and the reception hall plus ordering all flowers, corsages, etc., for everyone who needs them; you, Angie, will take care of the invitations, meal, cake, and liquor plans, but once you choose the caterers, baker, and bartender, you turn everything all over to Bianca to handle. Plus, you will oversee and agree or disagree with what everyone else comes up with. Anything you don't like will be changed. Now, stop fussing and start enjoying your wedding!"

Angie was flabbergasted. Cat didn't even ask if that was what she wanted or not. On the other hand, who knew her and her taste better than her sisters? Who could she more easily work with to get exactly what she wanted?

She looked at Cat and smiled for the first time. This wedding might actually happen...in only four months! "Thank you!"

The two then took off for the Bridal Boutique shop on Maiden Lane.

"Miss Amalfi!" the owner cried. "Thank goodness you're here!"

Really? Angie thought that was a strange thing to say. "Kellie, this is my sister, Caterina Swenson," Angie said. "She's going to help me."

"Another sister?" Kellie looked a little sick.

Now Angie was even more confused by the normally controlled woman.

"I'm so glad to meet—" Kellie began when Cat cut her off.

"I understand my sister liked a Vera Wang last time she was here. Can you show me the dress?"

"Yes. Right this way." Kellie led them back into the area where row after row of dresses hung on racks...and that was when Angie discovered why Kellie looked so stressed.

Over at the bridesmaids' dresses stood her mother and three sisters. Dresses were being pulled and tugged by the women, who were so engrossed arguing with each other they didn't even notice that Angie and Cat had arrived.

"Here's the dress Angie liked," Kellie said, taking one of the bride's dresses from the rack.

"Go ahead, Angie," Cat told her. "Try it on. I'll get the others to pay attention to what you'll be wearing instead of their own dresses."

Kellie helped her into the dress and pinned it so that the floor model fit her the way it should after alterations.

She stepped out into an area with a slightly raised platform, a half-circle of mirrors, and a place where the family sat. Her mother and all four sisters were sitting there, waiting for her to appear.

She felt like a bride for the first time as all of them oohed and aahed as she stepped onto the platform. In a matter of seconds, however, the cries turned negative.

"I see the problem," Cat announced. "The mermaid line looks best on someone tall. It seems to emphasize her shortness."

"She looks like a little kid playing dress-up," Bianca said.

"Dumpy," Frannie smirked.

"*Bellissima!*" Serefina cried. "But not right."

"Bleah!" was Maria's comment.

"What about that one," Angie pointed to another Vera Wang she thought was beautiful.

The second dress one didn't even get praise as she walked out of the dressing room.

"Nope, too poofy," Maria announced.

"Too much frou-frou on it," Cat said.

"*Bellissima!*" Serefina cried. "She looks like Cinderella going to the ball. But, maybe Cinderella isn't right for a wedding."

Frannie just looked at her, pointed, and laughed.

"Thanks loads," Angie said. This was like being stuck in a bridal intervention from hell. She liked both those dresses.

"Let's go step by step," Cat said. "What kind of bodice do you like?"

"Lots of detail."

"Strapless?"

"Not necessarily."

Cat faced the others. "No mermaid, no poofs, detailed bodice. Got it?"

While Serefina sat beside Angie, holding her hand, the sisters turned into whirling dervishes going through the sample dresses, pulling out and rejecting one after the other. Kellie tried to interfere a couple of times and soon learned her help wasn't needed and definitely not wanted. After about fifteen minutes of this, Frannie cried out "Ah ha!"

She pulled out a Lazaro crepe satin A-line gown with a silver embroidered overlay, jeweled bodice with a strapless curved neckline, and a sweep train. The embroidered overlay on the satin was highly detailed and quite gorgeous.

"Hmm," Bianca said, taking the dress from Frannie. "It's very traditional. The line is simple but elegant, the embroidery on the overlay is stunning.

"It reminds me of the dress Kate Middleton wore when she married into the British royal family," Cat said, "except that hers had long sleeves with lace up to her neck in front, and a somewhat different shape to it."

"And didn't have a silver embroidered overlay or jeweled bodice," Maria added.

"I'll try it on," Angie said.

After the fitters helped her into it, Angie had to blink a couple of times that it was really her. The long drop of the A-line gown against her slim form gave the impression of both elegance and height, and the magnificently jeweled and detailed bodice gave her relatively flat chest some depth. Even the train, which Angie didn't think she wanted, looked beautiful.

She stepped out of the dressing room and up onto the platform.

To her amazement, mother and sisters were completely silent.

Cat got up, lifted an eyebrow as she slowly walked all the way around. "What do you think, Angie?"

"It surprises me. It's nothing like what I thought I wanted."

"Do you like it?"

"I love it!"

"*Bellissima!* Ah, my baby is going to get married." Serefina said, then she started to cry. "I'm getting so old!"

The others burst into a cacophony of words about how beautiful the dress looked on her.

"Let's see it with a veil," Cat said to Kellie. "I'd like to see silk tulle with a trim of individual flowers hand-cut from lace. Something delicate, and that will look beautiful with a diamond comb to hold it in place."

Kellie raised her eyebrows a moment. "I know just the veil that will go perfectly with that dress. And I've got a small comb of fake diamonds to give you an idea of how it'll look." She dashed off to the back room.

"She'll need a diamond necklace with the dress," Bianca said. "I have one she can borrow."

"And I'll get her a blue garter," Frannie said with a wink.

Kellie came out with the veil and put it on Angie.

"I'll have to pin my hair back," Angie said.

"Of course," Cat replied. "The crowning glory, literally."

Angie had to agree. The dress was both demure because of its traditional lines, yet cut low enough, with material that clung close enough, to be sexy.

"It works. How much does the dress cost?" she asked.

"You don't want to know," Serefina said. "But Papà will be sure he paid for a quality dress for you."

Angie twisted and turned, tried walking, danced around the room by herself...everything was perfect. She loved everything about it, and couldn't remember ever seeing a dress so beautiful. "I love it. I want it!"

Cat looked at Kellie. "Sold. Also, my sister will need wedding shoes—four inch heels, platform soles, and why don't we have them custom made? I think white satin with lace hand embroidery would be excellent."

"Of course," Kellie said with a swallow. "I'll fit Angie for the shoes now."

"They'll be ready on time?"

"It should be no problem at all!" Kellie said.

"You're making this too easy," Angie said.

"It's hardly rocket science," Cat said.

The shoe fitting complete, Cat told Kellie all the sisters would be back in a few days to pick out the bridesmaids dresses.

Kellie struggled to find a smile and could only produce a sickly, "How wonderful."

Even Angie felt a bit sorry for her, knowing what the woman was going to have to deal with.

As they all stepped out of the store, Cat looked at Angie. "I have no idea why you were fussing so much about finding a dress. It was simple. You're such a drama queen, Angie!"

Finding the right wedding dress filled Angie with renewed energy and *joie de vivre*. She and her mother and sisters went out to lunch to discuss bridesmaid's dresses, and as Angie expected, each had a different opinion regarding color and style. Fun days ahead.

After lunch, Angie went home. She knew she should look at wedding invitations and party favors, table decorations and so forth, but she didn't feel like sitting.

No matter what she told herself she "should" do, she only wanted to do one thing. Finally, she gave into temptation.

She changed into a business-like gray Donna Karan suit with black Prada shoes and a black Gucci handbag. With them, she wore gold earrings, a necklace, and bracelet. She wanted to look like someone the administrator of Restful Gardens, where Carol Steed lived, would have no problem allowing inside to meet with a patient.

The administrator was a friendly, older woman. Angie stood straight, head high, and hoped the administrator would realize she wasn't there to try to scam anyone and handed her the note from Enid Norbel.

"I would gladly allow you to see Mrs. Steed," the administrator said. "But she isn't here at the moment. She's on home leave. She stopped in at eight a.m. for her pills, and will be here again at eight p.m. But other than that, she's home."

"She has that much freedom?" Angie asked.

"As long as she checks in with us every twelve hours to take her meds, which keep her every bit as healthy as you and I, and has a home care nurse with her at night, there's no reason not to allow her to go wherever she wants. This isn't a prison. Our residents have their rights."

Angie drove straight to 60 Clover Lane.

An elderly woman, tall, medium build, with short gray hair, opened the door and gave Angie a quick once-over. "I guess you Jehovah's Witnesses are coming up in the world," she said. "I'm an atheist." She stepped back to swing the door shut.

"Wait, please!" Angie put out her hand to stop the door. "This isn't about religion, and I'm not selling anything! My name is Angelina Amalfi. Are you Carol Steed?"

"Why do you want to know?"

"I spoke to your daughter, Enid, and she told me it would be all right to ask you about the house across the street."

Carol didn't smile. Her face sagged and her eyes were piercing. "Why? It's not for sale."

Uh oh, Angie thought. "I...I've heard some interesting things about it, that's all."

Carol snorted. "I imagine you have. People tried to lock me up because of that house. They say I see things."

She moved closer and dropped her voice. "They say I see ghosts in it. If I were you, unless you want everyone saying you're crazy the way they do me, forget you ever saw it."

The words were disturbing, but Angie reminded herself the woman was mentally ill. "I understand you once lived there. I'd like to talk to you about it if you have time."

"I don't mind, but I didn't live there for very long. Come on in." She led Angie to the living room.

The house was as tiny inside as it appeared from the street. The windows faced the ocean, providing a view that was the house's best feature.

As soon as they sat, Carol started talking again. "After Edward's mother passed away, we moved into the house. Edward had some remodeling done. Made it nicer. More modern."

"But then Edward died?"

Her mouth clamped shut a moment before she said, "Yes, he died."

"And you moved out of the house?"

Carol scowled. "How did you—?"

"Let's talk about what happened back then," Angie interrupted. "You rented it out, right?"

She thought a moment, then smiled. "To Eric. He loved it very much, you see. Loved the view. He said it was worth a million dollars just for the view. But I wouldn't sell it. No, sir!"

"And then?" Angie asked, doing her best to keep her voice and her expression soft, gentle, and encouraging—a veritable Diane Sawyer handling a delicate interview. "Your baby was born, right?"

Carol nodded. "Yes. Enid was born."

Angie drew in her breath. "What happened next?"

Carol's lips turned downward, and even after all these

years, Angie saw the emotion the memories caused her. "Eric brought home a wife. He had to marry her, he said. She pressured him, you know. He was very sorry. He told me that."

"Sorry for what?"

"It was long ago."

"You didn't like it that he brought another woman into your house, did you?"

She shrugged. "It wasn't my business. That's what she told me—that his marriage wasn't my business. The tart!"

"I can imagine how you must have felt," Angie said. "You must have hated her."

She watched the light go out of Carol Steed's eyes, as if she were shutting down. She tried a new tact. "Can you tell me anything about the house?"

"It's a beautiful house. Eric lives there." Then her eyes took on a crafty look, and she put her fingers up to her mouth. "Or...he did," she whispered.

"Things seem to move around strangely in that house. Did you ever see anything like that?"

She stared at the floor. "Of course not."

Angie leaned close and practically whispered, "You can trust me, Mrs. Steed. I wouldn't tell anyone."

"No! I've never seen anything!"

"But you used to tell people you saw ghosts."

"Me? Never!"

"What do you remember about the Flemings?"

"Nothing."

"Did you ever see any problem around them, see anyone threatening them, or anything like that?"

Carol remained still, not answering or moving.

Angie asked gently, "Did Edward ever haunt the house?"

"Edward? Did you say Edward? My husband?" Carol chortled. "He wouldn't have the balls."

"Who do you think is haunting it?"

Carol's gaze turned cold and black, and Angie had the feeling the madness had lifted and all that remained was pure malice. "No one, of course. There's no such thing as ghosts."

"But if someone were to, who would it be?"

"I suppose it would be Eric. He loved the house."

"Not his wife?"

"Wife! She was no wife to him! She had no business being with him! She never understood or loved him."

"Didn't they have a good marriage?"

Carol cocked her head. "If they had, he wouldn't have killed her, would he? She was a bitch in this life, I hate to think she's still making him miserable in the afterlife."

"I believe I've seen things moving around in the house where they lived," Angie said softly. "Haven't you seen such things, too?"

Carol's gaze hardened, and her lips spread into a creepy grin. "Oh? And have you also seen a unicorn in the garden?"

Angie decided it was time to leave. She considered leaving her phone number, but then a better thought struck. She reached into her purse, pulled out the small metal case that held her name and address cards—she had had them created for job interviews and still had a lot left. She handed it to Carol. "My business cards are inside if you'd like one. You can call me and we can talk."

Carol handed it back. "We've talked quite enough."

Angie dropped the case back into her purse. "Goodbye, Mrs. Steed." With that, she hurried from the house, glad to get away.

oOo

Angie went straight to Homicide to see Paavo. She hadn't wanted to involve him in 'her' murders, as she called them. But now, as far as she was concerned, she couldn't keep it to herself any longer.

"The murderer has to be Carol Steed, the owner of the Clover Lane house," Angie said as soon as she sat down. She was glad to find Paavo still at work. "She had access, opportunity, and motive. Everyone who knew Eric back then said he was quite the charmer as well as being smart and rich. He had lots of women around him. One of them was Carol Steed! They had an affair and she got pregnant. She gave her daughter a picture of Eric and said he was her father."

"Hold on, Angie," Paavo said. "I take it this is about Eric and Natalie Fleming?"

"Of course it is!" she said. "The motive was the hard part, but now it all makes sense. Carol Steed got rid of her husband of fourteen years. Maybe it can never be proved that she killed him, but even news reports of the time wrote that bad luck caused his head to hit a rock in just the way to cause a fatal injury. I suspect Carol hit him in the head—maybe with a rock or a brick or a swing of a shovel. Then he either fell off the cliff or she pushed him off."

"Wait..." He regarded her with a frown. "You're suggesting this Carol Steed actually killed three people?"

"Yes! That's what I'm trying to explain," Angie cried. Yosh heard this and turned around to listen. "Then, after Carol Steed killed her husband, she moved Eric Fleming into her house, probably expecting to live there with him," Angie said, summarizing the story. "But it never happened. Instead, Eric got married and stopped using drugs and drinking. That was bad enough, but I suspect Carol went completely over the edge when she learned that Eric and Natalie were moving to a house they were having built. Soon after that, they were both dead."

"So you're saying Carol Steed killed them out of jealousy," Paavo said.

"I think she did."

Paavo nodded. It all fit together. "Once the murder-suicide idea started to be pushed, it became a domestic dispute, and a low priority since both parties were dead. I imagine money was tight, and other, more pressing cases probably took over for attention. But the detectives were bothered enough that they put the case in the cold files, even though they had no physical proof of a third party being involved."

"That's what I suspect," Angie said. "I also wonder if that was why Carol named her child Enid. People might have thought she named her in honor of Edward, but the name is just as close to Eric. Oh—I almost forgot!" She carefully lifted her business card case from her purse and put it on Paavo's desk. "Carol's fingerprints are on this case, along with mine, in case you need them."

"I'll need a set of your prints before you leave," Paavo said, "to make it easier on the crime lab."

"Of course."

"You've turned into quite the investigator, Angie." Paavo used his handkerchief to lift the case into an evidence bag. "The lab can run these prints against whatever they might have from the original crime scene. Sounds like it's time to talk to Carol Steed. She's old and mentally unstable, but if she's also a murderer, she took away the lives of two young people who thought they had finally found happiness, and possibly her husband's as well. It's tragic."

"Yes," Angie said, "my thoughts, exactly."

"But unless we get a confession from Carol it's unlikely we'll be able to arrest her, let alone have the DA prosecute. Even then, a good defense lawyer would make mincemeat of a confession from an elderly, diagnosed schizophrenic. Absent physical evidence, she's home free."

"She'll get away with triple murder," Angie said in a grim voice. "Although, I think being mad is a terrible kind of punishment in itself."

Chapter 25

A S PAAVO WENT back to investigating the Wyndom and Bedford murders, he also thought about Angie's conviction that Carol Steed killed the Flemings out of jealousy. It was a plausible motive and a common one.

What made his murder cases strange was that the lovers, Marilee and Taylor, weren't the ones murdered. Instead, Gaia was a victim, which made no sense.

Clearly, Marilee and Gaia didn't like each other, but if every family member who didn't get along with others killed them, the country would be awash in blood.

Even if Marilee killed Gaia, he saw no reason for her to have killed Taylor. Marilee loved him. Gaia was the jealous one.

And he didn't believe two different murderers were involved.

He flipped through the case's files when something jumped out at him from Yosh's interview with the bartender.

He sat down at Yosh's desk to discuss his thoughts with his partner. Yosh agreed with the premise, but so far it was pure conjecture. They had no proof.

Before long, Yosh left for home. Paavo stayed to bring

Angie's business card case to the crime scene unit along with her set of fingerprints and the old case file from the Fleming murders. He explained to the crime scene technician that once he eliminated Angie's prints, those remaining belonged to Carol Steed.

The tech needed to see if Steed's prints had been found at the Fleming crime scene.

As he headed back to Homicide, he passed the forensics laboratory, which gave him an idea.

Before doing anything, he called Ray Larson in Jenner. The old man had been pretty proud of his observation skills. Paavo put them to a test.

Larson gave Paavo a quick answer.

Paavo then turned his step toward the Medical Examiner's office. Evelyn Ramirez was still at work. She seemed to put in even more hours on the job than he did.

He asked Ramirez to pull samples of Gaia's hair from hair brushes found in her house, and then samples of what had been determined to be Gaia's hair from the freezer.

The DNA of identical twins, like everything else about them, was essentially identical. Hair, however, was an exception. Hair was made from protein, metabolized amino acids from the foods eaten. As hair grew, it became a record of the amino acids that had been used in its creation.

In that way, the protein in hair gave a history of the diet of the person whose hair was studied. Not only could foods from a marine vs. a terrestrial environment be identified, but also the kinds of terrestrial plants, complex proteins and meats eaten could be determined.

"I'm desperate, Evelyn," he said. "I'd like a forensic hair analysis on follicles from both samples."

"Why?" Ramirez asked.

"Gaia was a vegetarian. I've been told her sister was not."

Ramirez raised her eyebrows. "I see. It's worth a try."

She agreed to get on it right away. She warned him that the analysis might take some time to complete.

Back at his desk, Paavo leaned back in his chair, hands intertwined behind his head. Both Gaia Wyndom and Carol Steed were loners, intelligent, unhappy with their lives, and potentially mentally ill. People around them knew they needed help, but didn't know how to give it to them without their consent. They hadn't done anything illegal as far as others knew—even though some may have held the unspoken suspicion that Gaia had been behind her parents' deaths, and Carol behind her husband's.

Because of their intelligence, they were able to come up with plans that allowed them to get away with murder...almost.

Years ago, before his job took away most of his free time, Paavo had been a voracious reader. He thought now of the first line from *Anna Karenina,* which he read as a young man trying to understand families and women since he grew up pretty well isolated from both. It said, "All happy families are alike; each unhappy family is unhappy in its own way."

And those were both very unhappy families.

The next day, a little before noon, Paavo received the results of the analysis from Dr. Ramirez. She must have stayed up all night running the test. He owed her, big time.

He and Yosh drove to Marilee's cabin in Lagunitas.

Marilee let them into the house and immediately began to scoop up the cats from the great room.

"You don't have to shut them away," Paavo said.

"Those are Gaia's cats, aren't they?"

"No," Marilee said.

"Gaia loved her cats. Everyone said so. Her vet told us they were two little gray and white tuxedo cats, brothers, eight-years old. She wouldn't have left them alone and unfed even if she had committed suicide. She never would have hurt them, and I can't see her giving them away."

Marilee put them in the back porch and shut the door, then turned towards Paavo, arms folded. "Those are my cats and no one else's!"

"The cats have microchips in them. Something tells me the chips in those cats would match Gaia's."

Her voice turned low and lethal. "You will not touch my cats! What is this about?"

Paavo went over to the sofa and sat.

Yosh quietly backed up to a wall out of Marilee's line of vision, folded his arms, and listened.

"Did you know," Paavo began, "that Gaia was in love with Taylor?"

Marilee gave a harsh, hacking laugh, then sat in a stiff-backed chair facing him. "Love? Childish infatuation was more like it. Anyway, I'm the one who told you about it, if I remember correctly."

"You said he once tried to kiss her in the office. Of course, he immediately knew she wasn't you."

Her eyes hardened. "I never said that. And anyway, who cares? Why are you bothering me with this old news, Inspector?"

"Taylor could never be fooled by Gaia pretending to be you," Paavo said. "Everyone who knew her said Gaia was just about the most boring woman they had ever come across, while everyone who knew you, Marilee, said you were vivacious and fun. You have imagination. Look at your books, your house. The art work you have here, the sculptures. Everything about you reeks of interest and of life. Gaia could never fool anyone that she was you."

Marilee's face reddened. She stood. "I'm sure she never tried to! Now, I'd like you to leave, Inspector."

"Actually, you're wrong," Paavo said, leaning back with his arm flung across the back of the sofa. "Taylor told a friend that Gaia once pretended to be Marilee. Taylor said he found her pathetic and disgusting."

"No!"

"Yes! He knew. That weekend at the beach cabin—the last weekend he was alive—Gaia was there instead of you. She pretended to be you, but even she knew she couldn't pull it off. Taylor left a day early, on Saturday instead of Sunday. He was so upset that instead of going home, he went to his favorite bar in the Financial District. His usual bartender wasn't there that night, so he had no one to tell exactly what had happened. But he didn't need to tell anyone because his actions said it all. He left the cabin, left Gaia alone. Anyone of us could put two-and-two together and understand how Taylor felt about Gaia trying to fool him."

"No!" Marilee screamed.

"He must have found her pathetic. He probably hated Gaia then, swore he would have her fired. She'd lose him and everything that meant anything to her."

Yosh walked into the great room from the kitchen area. "No meat," he said.

Marilee spun around to face him, as if she'd forgotten he was there.

"No meat in the refrigerator?" Paavo said. "How can that be, when everyone knows Marilee likes meat? She and Taylor often grilled sausages, hotdogs, and big juicy hamburgers at the beach house."

"I've decided to eat healthier," Marilee said, backing away from Yosh as her eyes darted between the two detectives.

"Oh? Since when?" Paavo asked. "Since two weeks ago?"

She slowly sat down again, her voice little more than a whisper. "No, that's not true."

"It is true. Gaia pretended to be Marilee with Taylor. Not only that, but she moved here, into your house, used your shampoos, wore your clothes, burned your incense. Then she went to the cabin and met Taylor. But smells and clothes weren't enough. He left.

"Somehow Gaia convinced him to meet her in San Francisco—maybe by pretending to be Marilee again, maybe telling him crazy Gaia might harm them both. However she did it, she convinced him to meet her in an alley. There, still pretending to be Marilee, Gaia threw herself in his arms, and then stabbed him. She was a big woman, and she was strong."

"How terrible of her!" Marilee's chest heaved with emotion. She turned pale and appeared faint. "I always knew something was wrong with her, but I didn't think it was that serious."

"That isn't the half of it," Paavo said. "Looking back at what happened to your parents, I can't help but wonder about their accident."

Marilee's eyes widened. "My parents?"

"In Gaia's home, we could find no photos, photo albums, or anything else about your parents, as if she wanted to erase them from her mind. Your parents were killed when their car went out of control on the way home from Jenner, but your father was a slow and cautious driver, and he knew that road well. The car caught fire, so little was done to investigate the accident. Was it truly an accident, or had the car been tampered with?"

When she didn't answer, he continued. "We also know that Gaia hated Marilee. I wondered how every trace of 'Urda' had been eliminated from government databases, until I learned that Thomas Greenburg had first been known as a hacker. He could hack into anything—including government databases. Gaia gave him $300,000 to obliterate any trace of Urda. That's a lot of hatred. It was odd, everyone said, how simple Gaia's job was at Zygog, and that she was one of the few people allowed to come and go as she wished there."

"I know nothing about that," she said.

He stood. "You should...because you're Gaia. You hated Marilee, hated having an identical twin who was more liked, more loved, more *alive* than you had ever been. Both of you lived in a symbiosis of hate. Intimate hate."

She clutched the chair arms. "No, you've got it all wrong!"

He paced as he spoke. "The way I see it, Marilee began all this as a grand joke on a hated twin. First she stole the man you loved. You must have decided you could make it work for you at first, since you cut your hair to look like Marilee's. Maybe because Taylor now paid some attention to you at work—you shared secret smiles or whatever. It was more than you ever had in your life, and it might have been enough."

The woman bowed her head, shut her eyes, and covered her face with her hands. "It's not true," she whispered.

"Two weeks ago, everything changed. Maybe what started out as a joke turned into love for Marilee as well.

What happened, Gaia? Did she tell you she planned to confess everything to Taylor? Tell him she wasn't the woman he worked with, but an identical twin sister? You knew that once she did, Taylor wouldn't care about you any longer, and your quiet, secret little love life would fall apart. But Marilee, who you hated, would be happy."

Paavo continued, "You couldn't have that. You bought the freezer, invited Marilee to your house, and probably slipped her enough sleeping pills to subdue her so you could then force her to take a lethal dose. You put her in the freezer, and probably would have left her there except for one thing. When you went to the cabin to meet Taylor, he knew something was terribly wrong. You weren't the woman he loved. He returned to San Francisco, troubled and confused. You knew he would start asking questions. Evidence that you had a twin, and that you killed her, could eventually come out. So you had no choice but to kill Taylor as well.

"You could have gone on, gone back to living as Gaia and probably it would have been damned difficult to figure out who killed Taylor. But you hated your life, and had always envied your sister's. So you decided to become Marilee. You put Marilee into a hot tub of water where her frozen corpse defrosted. That was why the medical examiner had such a difficult time assessing the time of death. You knew that eventually someone would look for Gaia and find her body.

"But you couldn't leave your cats to starve. You brought them here."

Yosh stepped a bit closer, ready to move if she tried to escape.

Paavo stood. "Gaia Wyndom, you're under arrest for the murders of Marilee Wisdom, aka Urda Lee Wyndom, and Taylor Bedford. You have the right to remain silent..."

"No!" she screamed over Paavo's statement of her rights. "It's not true! I'm not Gaia! I'm Marilee!"

When he finished the Miranda rights, he added, "An analysis of hair shows that the person found dead in the bathtub was a meat eater, while you, Gaia, proudly proclaim yourself a vegetarian. Now that you're under arrest, we'll have your fingerprints. Identical twins don't have the same fingerprints. Your deception will be unmasked. You can count on it. Let's go." Paavo took her arm, making her stand, and hand-cuffed her.

"Wait!" She looked around, wild-eyed. "You can't do this! What about my cats? They need me!"

He hustled her out the door.

"They need me!" she cried, with tears running down her cheeks.

"We'll take care of them," he said.

"No! Don't give them to the Humane Society. What if no one wants them? They'll kill them!"

"You should have thought of that before you murdered two people," he said as he pushed her into the back of the car.

From time to time, Paavo had talked to Angie about being on a stake-out. His main recommendations were to drink little water, have some strong coffee on hand in case you get sleepy, and food in case you get hungry.

As she drove to the house at 51 Clover Lane, she had filled her tote with a thermos of espresso, a packet of almonds, five varieties of energy bars, two apples, homemade chocolate chip cookies, Doritos, two types of Cadbury bars, plus crossword puzzles and Sudokus. After her visit to Carol Steed, she had a strong feeling that she needed to keep an eye on the woman.

She might be crazy, but she wasn't stupid and might have figured out what Angie was up to.

Angie unlocked the door and walked into the house.

The furniture had been haphazardly moved around. A dead mouse lay in a candy dish on the coffee table—not the candy dish she had replaced. That one was gone. She had seen this dish in Carol Steed's living room.

She wondered if Carol thought she wouldn't recognize it, or if Carol purposefully tried to intimidate her.

Or had these actions been designed to make Angie think the house was haunted? To get her to abandon her wish to buy the house?

For all she knew, Carol Steed had been watching her come and go from the house all week, and decided to scare her off. Carol surely still had a key to the house. Very likely, she had broken the candy dish and even knocked over the vase in the living room while Angie and Stan were out on the back deck!

She had probably scared off all earlier prospective buyers as well. Angie heaved a sigh of relief. She told herself not to worry any longer about the occult or the supernatural. Everything had been caused by one crazy old woman filled with guilt and madness.

Even as she tried to convince herself of that, however, some events weren't explainable.

Angie decided to simply ignore them.

She picked up the candy dish and put it and the dead mouse out in the back yard. When she came back in, she made sure she locked the sliding glass door. Then she opened the garage door and drove her Mercedes inside, shutting the door behind it. That way, unless Carol had been sitting at the window and saw her pull in, she wouldn't know Angie was there.

Angie went through the house, checking and double-checking that all doors and windows were locked, and then pushed a chair in front of the window in the den. It faced the street, and Carol Steed's home.

Now that she was set up for her vigil, Angie phoned Paavo. He picked up on the first ring—a rarity.

"Guess where I am?" she said.

"Do I have to?"

"I'm in the Sea Cliff on a stakeout."

"Stakeout?" Paavo's voice was a mix of long-suffering and gloom.

"I'm convinced that Carol's been coming in here to sabotage a sale, and I want to catch her. Anyone who puts a dead mouse in a candy dish deserves to be caught."

"I don't want to know about any dead mice. What I do know is that you shouldn't be confronting a crazy woman who may be a murderer."

"Well...maybe I need my favorite detective on stakeout with me. I've got goodies."

"I'm sure you do. And you should take them and yourself home. Now."

"You worry too much."

"With good reason! Anyway, I just made an arrest in my double homicide. I've got a few more things to wrap up and I'll be there. Be careful. Take no chances."

"You know me, I'm always careful."

"Since when?"

"I'll be waiting," she said with a big smile as she hung up.

Two hours later, she realized how incredibly boring this stake-out business could be. She had worked two crosswords and three Sudokus, ate an apple, an energy bar, half the packet of almonds, and drank the equivalent of three espressos. The candy and cookies were calling to her, but so far, she had succeeded in saving them for Paavo. All in all, this might be a waste of time. She had just about decided to go home when she heard a noise in the house, and what sounded like footsteps on the hardwood floor.

Footsteps that were coming closer...

After he finished processing Gaia Wyndom and explaining the case to the District Attorney, Paavo returned to Homicide.

He found a report from the crime scene technician. Few prints had been found at the crime scene, and none matched Carol Steed's. He expected that the original homicide inspectors would have discovered it if the landlady's prints had been found at the crime scene.

Despite that, he found Angie's arguments convincing. He wanted to talk to Carol Steed, and phoned the mental institution listed as her residence.

He was told she remained on home leave as Angie suspected.

Since this was a cold case, he telephoned Lt. Eastwood to explain what he was doing and that he planned to reopen the case. He got Eastwood's voice mail.

He didn't like waiting, but after all, the case had sat in storage, unresolved for thirty years. What difference could a few more minutes make?

Angie peeked out of the den. She didn't see anyone in the living or dining rooms.

She put on her jacket, stuffed the food, thermos, and puzzles back into her tote bag, grabbed her purse, and hurried across the living room to the kitchen and through the mudroom.

She swung open the door to the garage and saw Carol Steed standing in front of her car. She held a revolver. "Going somewhere?" Carol asked.

Angie slammed the door shut and started to run, then reached back and turned the deadbolt just as a gunshot created a hole in the door, missing Angie by inches. Now, she did run, sure Carol would have a key to the lock.

Back in the living room, Angie heard the whirr of the automatic garage door opener. Carol must be expecting her to go out the front door, to try to reach neighbors, other people. If she ran out to the front of the house, Carol would gun her down.

Instead, she dropped her belongings and fled out the sliding glass door to the back yard.

She ran toward the fence. It was about four and a half feet tall; high enough to keep small children in, but not so high as to obscure the ocean view. Somehow, she'd have to climb over it. She wasn't much of a climber, but knowing a crazy person with a gun stalked her, despite the smooth leather platform soles on her high-heel boots, she scrambled up and over it.

She crouched down and snuck along the side of the fence toward the cliff. Everything in her wanted to go in the direction of the street instead, but she believed Carol waiting for her there.

She hoped to find a place to hide somewhere along the very backside of the fence where it ran along the cliff's edge. But Paavo had said he would try to get there soon. He'd see the garage door open, Angie's car inside it. He'd see the open sliding glass door.

But would he see Carol and her gun?

What if he didn't? What if came here concentrating on

finding Angie and because of that, he got shot...or worse? She had to go back, had to find a way to warn him and make sure he was safe.

She froze, torn by what to do, which way to run, when the choice was made for her.

Paavo parked in front of Carol Steed's house at 60 Clover Lane. He had grown tired of waiting for Eastwood's approval and decided to talk to Steed on his own—no harm in talking to someone.

As he walked up to the front door, rang the bell and knocked, he saw the open garage door across the street at 51 Clover, Angie's car inside. He shook his head. Despite his warnings, he could well imagine her wanting a front row seat to watch Carol Steed's possible arrest.

No answer. He knocked again, but the results were no better.

Carol Steed held the gun on Angie. "Why did you have to get involved in all this? Everything was fine in my life, and then you started prying."

Angie stood, her hands raised. "Please put the gun down, Mrs. Steed. We need to talk."

"I want you to walk towards the cliff."

Angie backed up a few steps, as directed, then stopped. "I thought you loved Eric. Why did you kill him?"

Carol's brows tightened, her face filled with emotion for a second or two, then she regained control. "He wouldn't give her up!" she cried. "He was young, and so foolish!"

"It must have been hard on you," Angie said, trying to control the shaking of her voice.

"I wanted Eric to tell Natalie that he loved me, to tell

her that Enid was our child. He refused. He married her only because she was rich, you know. He loved me, and would always love me. But he wouldn't explain that to her! No matter what I said, he wouldn't tell her he loved me."

"You made them walk out here to the cliff?" she asked.

"I told him I'd made a mistake, loving him, doing everything for him! I even got rid of Edward. Poor Edward. But Eric and I loved each other. We lived together until he brought Natalie into my house! Then, I was supposed to go back to the little shack, stay out of his life. Even after he'd gotten married, he'd come to visit me now and then. He'd play with Enid. But then, he said he and his rich wife were building a big house. He would leave me. He told me it was better that way.

"I couldn't stand it! I couldn't bear to lose him. I put my gun to his head. Oh, he told me he loved me then! Yes, he swore it. He told Natalie everything—how he loved me and Enid, how he would stay with us, divorce her. But then he told her I'd killed Edward!"

Angie blanched hearing that. She guessed what was coming.

"I knew, then, he was lying to me. He tried to warn her—that if I'd killed once, I might do it again. He thought lying to me would placate me. That I might let them go! He was wrong. I couldn't let them live—not either of them. If I did, they'd have me arrested. They'd take me away from Enid. I had to raise her. She needed her mother....

"So I pulled the trigger. There was so much blood! It splashed in my eyes, blinding me. I saw Natalie running and I fired again and again. She fell. I carefully wiped the gun everywhere I could think of, then put it in Eric's hand, pressing his fingers to it, and went home."

"But his car," Angie said. "How did it end up at the

Russian River?"

"I wasn't thinking. I went home and took a shower. Then I packed a bag for me and Enid, got into Eric's car and headed north. I wanted to go to Canada. But then, just a couple of hours from home, I started to wonder. What if the Canadian border guards checked the car registration? What if word got out that Eric was dead? I realized that being caught with his car would be a confession of guilt. So I hid it as best I could. Then Enid and I hitch-hiked to a Greyhound bus station and took the bus back to San Francisco. It took three days before the police came knocking on my door. They were easily fooled. But you weren't." Carol's attention focused on Angie. "You seemed a nice enough young woman. Too bad you don't mind your own business. Now, back up a little more."

Carol walked towards her and Angie had no choice but to back away from the gun pointed at her, closer and closer to the cliff.

Angie stopped, her heels on the edge of the land. Past her, it sloped rapidly downward. "Please," she said. "There's no reason for this."

Carol looked past Angie towards the ocean, her brow knitted. "Eric?"

Then she shook her head, as if forcing away the vision. Her gaze fixed again on Angie. She raised her gun as if to take aim.

A small white dog ran at her, barking and growling loudly. She turned her head as the dog lunged, its teeth clamping onto her ankle. "Stop it!" she shrieked, trying to shake the dog off, but it kept coming back. She turned the gun from Angie towards the dog, trying to get it in her sights, but it wriggled and jumped, still biting at her ankles and legs.

Angie saw her chance and threw herself at Carol's arm, knocking against it just as Carol pulled the trigger. The shot went wild. The force of Angie's tackle caused Carol to fall over. Angie landed on top of her. Carol was much bigger, but also much older. Angie had one hand on Carol's wrist with the gun, using her body weight to hold it down, and with the other hand she grabbed Carol's hair, tugging on it to lift Carol's head and then slam it down to the ground, hoping to somehow knock the woman out or at least stun her. Carol went from trying to push Angie away, to holding her wrist, and trying to pull Angie's hand free of her hair. But Angie held it in a death grip, knowing if she let go, Carol might kill her.

Suddenly, the gun was no longer in Carol's hand, and strong arms reached around Angie, lifting her and telling her everything was all right, she could stop now.

Paavo kept an arm around Angie, his 9mm automatic aimed at Carol, who was holding her head and woozily trying to sit up. Sirens, signaling the backup Paavo had called, shrieked towards them. Angie slumped against him, scarcely able to hold herself up another moment.

"Let's go," Paavo said, walking Angie towards her car after turning Carol Steed over to police custody. "Yosh is on his way. He'll take over for me here. In the meantime, you can wait in your car, and then I'll take you home."

"Not in the car," she said, brushing dust, dirt, and leaves off of her clothes and hair. She knew she would have very sore muscles tomorrow, but for the moment, she felt fine. "I want to go into the house. I'll be comfortable there, and safe."

He glanced at her with surprise. "Into the house? I

thought you'd never want to have anything to do with that house or this area again."

Angie knew what had happened out on the cliff, how she had been saved, but she also knew she could never explain it to Paavo or to anyone else unless she wanted to share adjoining padded cells with Carol Steed.

She walked with him through the garage into the house. An odd sense filled her of being welcomed and protected. The rational part of her said such good feelings were probably a mixture of adrenaline and pride over managing to wrestle a mad woman to the ground. After all, nobody had been shot or killed. The irrational part said much more was going on here.

The sliding glass door in the living room had been left open and she shut it after a quick look outside at the back yard, and the view beyond. It was a lovely sight. She decided a little white lie would explain a lot, and do more good than harm. "Carol Steed kept coming into the house, doing things here that made it feel as if some occult presence was involved. But there wasn't. It's just a house, Paavo. A lovely house."

He put his arms around her and studied her. "Are you sure you're all right? Do you want to see a doctor?"

"I'm fine." She looked up at him with love. They had a lot still to work out—minor, unimportant details about their wedding, and more important issues such as his ongoing relationship with Katie and Micky Kowalski. But she had faith that everything would turn out well in the end. "I'm glad we now know what happened to the two people who once lived here, and that they can finally have peace."

"They?" Paavo's arms tightened around her. "Well, if there are such things as ghosts, I agree that they should be happy that the truth has finally come out. Maybe they'll go off to wherever it is that ghosts go off to."

"I imagine they'll do exactly that." Angie put her arms around his neck. She was about to kiss him when from the corner of her eye she noticed something white in the back yard. She turned her head to see a little white Scottie dog sitting out there looking in at her.

She smiled. *Or*, she thought, *maybe not.*

From the Kitchen of Angelina Amalfi

ANGIE'S BAKED CHICKEN KIEV

Note that Chicken Kiev is usually deep-fried, but if you're watching your weight, like Angie, you might prefer to use this recipe.

6 Tbsp. butter, softened
1 Tbsp. chopped fresh parsley
½ tsp. leaf tarragon, crumbled
2 garlic cloves, finely minced
¼ tsp. salt
1/8 tsp. pepper
3 whole chicken breasts (6 halves—about 2 ½ lbs.)

Coating:
½ cup unseasoned bread crumbs
2 Tbsp. flour
1 egg
2 Tbsp. sesame seeds
Salt & pepper to taste

Preheat oven to 425 degrees Fahrenheit.

Combine butter, parsley, tarragon, garlic, salt and pepper in a bowl. Roll into 6 individual pieces. Place in refrigerator to chill, about 15 minutes until butter is firm.

If using whole chicken breasts, split in half; remove bones and skin. Place each piece between 2 pieces of waxed paper and flatten with wooden mallet or rolling pin. Remove parsley-butter from refrigerator. Place each roll of seasoned butter in center of each flattened chicken breast. Fold long side of chicken over butter, then fold ends over, being sure butter is completely covered. Fasten with wooden toothpicks.

Place flour on a sheet of waxed paper. Beat egg in a small bowl. In another bowl, combine bread crumbs, sesame seeds and salt and pepper to taste. Roll and cover each piece of chicken with flour, then egg, then bread crumb mixture. Coat completely.

Bake 5 minutes at 425 degrees, then lower heat to 400 degrees, and bake 25 minutes longer. Outside should be golden and crisp.

(Angie often drizzles a bit of melted butter over the chicken before serving.)

SPAGHETTI CARBONARA

¼ lb. pancetta diced (if not available, use 1/4 lb. bacon, diced)
1 Tbsp. olive oil
1 white onion, chopped
1 clove garlic minced
¼ cup dry white wine (optional)
1 lb. spaghetti
1 Tbsp. olive oil
4 eggs
½ cup grated Parmesan cheese
2 Tbsp. fresh parsley, chopped
1 large leaf basil, chopped fine
Salt & pepper to taste

In a large skillet, add oil, chopped pancetta (or bacon) and onion. Cook until pancetta is slightly crisp and onion translucent. Add garlic and wine and cook 1 minute more. Remove from heat.

Cook spaghetti in boiling water with 1 Tbsp. olive oil until al dente (8-10 minutes).

While spaghetti is cooking, in large bowl combine eggs, Parmesan cheese, parsley, basil, salt and pepper to taste. As soon as spaghetti is cooked, drain thoroughly, and toss hot spaghetti into bowl. Toss to coat spaghetti with mixture.

Reheat pancetta and as soon as skillet is hot, add spaghetti. Toss to mix in pancetta and to cook the egg. Serve.

(Angie sometimes sprinkles red pepper flakes on her carbonara at the table to add a little zest—but not too much or it'll overwhelm the subtle flavor of the carbonara.)

HARD, ROUND ICED ITALIAN COOKIES

Like Angie's Mamma makes...

½ lb. butter, softened
1 cup sugar
2 large eggs, beaten
1 Tbsp. vanilla
1 Tbsp. anise extract
4 cups flour
2 Tbsp. baking powder

Icing:
1 ¾ cup powdered sugar
1 Tbsp. anise extract (or 1 Tbsp. vanilla or 1 Tbsp. fresh lemon juice)
2 Tbsp. milk
Colored sugar for decoration

Preheat oven to 375 degrees Fahrenheit.

Cream butter and sugar until soft. Add eggs, vanilla and anise flavorings. Mix well. Combine flour and baking powder, then blend into the butter mixture.

Break off small, tablespoon size pieces of dough, roll and then twist into a circle, lightly pinching ends to stick together. (Can twist into any shape you like, bows, braids, "s" etc.) Bake 375 degrees until lightly browned, 15-20 minutes.

Icing: Blend sugar and flavoring, slowly add milk to form soft, smooth icing. Ice cookies when they cool off a bit. Sprinkle with colored sugar before icing sets.

About the Author

Joanne Pence was born and raised in northern California. She has been an award-winning, *USA Today* best-selling author of mysteries for many years, but she has also written suspense, historical fiction, contemporary romance, romantic suspense, and fantasy. All of her books are now available as e-books, and most are also in print.

Joanne hopes you'll enjoy her books, which present a variety of times, places, and reading experiences, from mysterious to thrilling, emotional to lightly humorous, as well as powerful tales of times long past.

Visit her at www.joannepence.com.

Ancient Echoes

Over two hundred years ago, a covert expedition shadowing Lewis and Clark disappeared in the wilderness of Central Idaho. Now, seven anthropology students and their professor vanish in the same area. The key to finding them lies in an ancient secret, one that men throughout history have sought to unveil.

Michael Rempart is a brilliant archeologist with a colorful and controversial career, but he is plagued by a sense of the supernatural and a spiritual intuitiveness. Joining Michael are a CIA consultant on paranormal phenomena, a washed-up local sheriff, and a former scholar of Egyptology. All must overcome their personal demons as they attempt to save the students and learn the expedition's terrible secret.

Seems Like Old Times

When Lee Reynolds, nationally known television news anchor, returns to the small town where she was born to sell her now-vacant childhood home, little does she expect to find that her first love has moved back to town. Nor does she expect that her feelings for him are still so strong.

Tony Santos had been a major league baseball player, but now finds his days of glory gone. He's gone back home to raise his young son as a single dad.

Both Tony and Lee have changed a lot. Yet, being with him, she finds that in her heart, it seems like old times...

Dance With A Gunfighter

Gabriella Devere wants vengeance. She grows up quickly when she witnesses the murder of her family by a gang of outlaws, and vows to make them pay for their crime. When the law won't help her, she takes matters into her own hands.

Jess McLowry left his war-torn Southern home to head West, where he hired out his gun. When he learns what happened to Gabriella's family, and what she plans, he knows a young woman like her will have no chance against the outlaws, and vows to save her the way he couldn't save his own family.

But the price of vengeance is high and Gabriella's willingness to sacrifice everything ultimately leads to the book's deadly and startling conclusion.

This is a harsh and gritty tale of the old West, in the tradition of Charles Portis' *True Grit* and Nancy Turner's *These is My Words*.

The Ghost of Squire House

For decades, the home built by reclusive artist, Paul Squire, has stood empty on a windswept cliff overlooking the ocean. Those who attempted to live in the home soon fled in terror. Jennifer Barrett knows nothing of the history of the house she inherited. All she knows is she's glad for the chance to make a new life for herself.

It's Paul Squire's duty to rid his home of intruders, but something about this latest newcomer's vulnerable status...and resemblance of someone from his past...dulls his resolve. Jennifer would like to find a real flesh-and-blood man to liven her days and nights—someone to share her life with—but living in the artist's house, studying his paintings, she is surprised at how close she feels to him.

A compelling, prickly ghost with a tortured, guilt-ridden past, and a lonely heroine determined to start fresh, find themselves in a battle of wills and emotion in this ghostly fantasy of love, time, and chance.

Gold Mountain

Against the background of San Francisco at the time of the Great Earthquake and Fire of 1906 comes a tale of love and loss. Ruth Greer, wealthy daughter of a shipping magnate, finds a young boy who has run away from his home in Chinatown—an area of gambling parlors, opium dens, sing-song girls, as well as families trying to eke out a living. It is also home to a number of highbinder tongs, the infamous "hatchet men" of Chinese lore.

There, Ruth meets the boy's father, Li Han-lin, the handsome, enigmatic leader of one such tong, and discovers he is neither as frightening, cruel, or wanton as reputation would have her believe. As Ruth's fascination with the area grows, she finds herself pulled deeper into the intrigue of the lawless area, and Han-lin's life. But the two are from completely different worlds, and when both worlds are shattered by the earthquake and fire that destroys San Francisco, they face their ultimate test.

Dangerous Journey

C.J. Perkins is trying to find her brother who went missing while on a Peace Corps assignment in Asia. All she knows is that the disappearance has something to do with a "White Dragon." Darius Kane, adventurer and bounty hunter, seems to be her only hope, and she practically shanghais him into helping her.

With a touch of the romantic adventure film Romancing the Stone, C.J. and Darius follow a trail that takes them through the narrow streets of Hong Kong, the backrooms of San Francisco's Chinatown, and the wild jungles of Borneo as they pursue both her brother and the White Dragon. The closer C.J. gets to them, the more danger she finds herself in—and it's not just danger of losing her life, but also of losing her heart.

[This is a completely revised author's edition of novel previously published as *Armed and Dangerous*.]

The Angie Amalfi Mysteries

Gourmet cook, sometime food columnist, sometime restaurant critic, and generally "underemployed" person Angelina Amalfi burst upon the mystery scene in SOMETHING'S COOKING, in which she met San Francisco Homicide Inspector Paavo Smith. Since that time—over the course of 14 books and a novella—she's wanted two things in life, a good job...and Paavo.

Here's a brief outline of each book in the order written:

Something's Cooking

For sassy and single food writer Angie Amalfi, life's a banquet—until the man who's been contributing unusual recipes for her food column is found dead. But Angie is hardly one to simper in fear—so instead she simmers over the delectable homicide detective assigned to the case.

Too Many Cooks

In TOO MANY COOKS, Angie's talked her way into a job on a pompous, third-rate chef's radio call-in show. But when a successful and much envied restaurateur is poisoned, Angie finds the case far more interesting than trying to make her pretentious boss sound good.

Cooking Up Trouble

Angie Amalfi's latest job, developing the menu for a new inn, sounds enticing—especially since it means spending a week in scenic Northern California with her homicide-detective boyfriend. But once she arrives at the soon-to-be-opened Hill Haven Inn, she's not so sure anymore. The added ingredients of an ominous treat, a missing person, and a woman making eyes at her man leave Angie convinced that the only recipe in this inn's kitchen is one for disaster.

Cooking Most Deadly

Food columnist Angie Amalfi has it all. But while she's wondering if it's time to cut the wedding cake with her boyfriend, Paavo, he becomes obsessed with a grisly homicide that has claimed two female victims. Angie becomes the next target of a vendetta that stretches from the dining rooms of San Francisco's elite to the seedy Tenderloin.

Cook's Night Out

Angie has decided to make her culinary name by creating the perfect chocolate confection: angelinas. Donating her delicious rejects to a local mission, Angie soon finds that the mission harbors more than the needy, and to save not only her life, but Paavo's as well, she's going to have to discover the truth faster than you can beat egg whites to a peak.

Cooks Overboard

Angie Amalfi's long-awaited vacation with her detective boyfriend has all the ingredients of a romantic getaway—a sail to Acapulco aboard a freighter, no crowds, no Homicide Department worries, and a red bikini. But it isn't long before Angie's *Love Boat* fantasies are headed for stormy seas—the cook tries to jump off the ship, Paavo is acting mighty strange, and someone's added murder to the menu...

A Cook In Time

Angie Amalfi has a way with food and people, but her newest business idea is turning out to be shakier than a fruit-filled gelatin mold. Now, her first—and only—clients for "Fantasy Dinners" are none other than a group of UFO chasers and government conspiracy fanatics. But when it seems that the group has a hidden agenda greater than anything on the *X-Files*, Angie's determined to find out the truth before it takes her out of this world...for good.

To Catch A Cook

Between her latest "sure-fire" foray into the food industry—video restaurant reviews—and her concern over Paavo's depressed state, Angie's plate is full to overflowing. Paavo has never come to terms with the fact that his mother abandoned him when he was four, leaving behind only a mysterious present. But when the token disappears, Angie discovers a lethal goulash of intrigue, betrayal, and mayhem that may spell disaster for her and Paavo.

Bell, Cook, and Candle

For once, Angie's newest culinary venture, "Comical Cakes," seems to be a roaring success! But there's nothing funny about her boyfriend Paavo's latest case—a series of baffling murders that may be rooted in satanic ritual. And it gets harder to focus on pastry alone when strange "accidents" and desecrations to her baked creations begin occurring with frightening regularity—leaving Angie to wonder whether she may end up as devil's food of a different kind.

If Cooks Could Kill

Angie Amalfi's culinary adventures always seem to fall flat, so now she's decided to cook up something different: love. But her earnest attempts at matchmaking don't go so well—her friend Connie is stood up by a no-show jock. Now Connie's fallen for a tarnished loner, and soon finds herself in the middle of a murder investigation. Angie's determined to find the real killer, but when the trail leads to the kitchen of her favorite restaurant, she fears she's about to discover a family recipe that dishes out disaster...and murder!

Two Cooks A-Killing

Angie hates to leave the side of her hunky fiancé, Paavo, but she gets an offer she can't refuse. She'll be preparing the banquet for her favorite soap opera's reunion special, on the estate where the show was originally filmed! But when a corpse turns up in the mansion's cellar, and Angie starts snooping around to investigate a past on-set death, she discovers that real-life events may be even more theatrical than the soap's on-screen drama.

Courting Disaster

Against her instincts, Angie agrees to let her control-freak mother plan her engagement party—she's just too busy to do it herself. And Angie's even more swamped when murder enters the picture. Now she must follow the trail of a mysterious pregnant kitchen helper at a nearby Greek eatery—a woman who her friendly neighbor Stan is infatuated with. And when Angie gets a little too close to the action, it looks like her fiancé Paavo may end up celebrating solo, after the untimely d.o.a. of his hapless fiancé!

Red Hot Murder

Angie and Paavo have had enough familial input regarding their upcoming wedding to last a lifetime. So Angie leaps at the chance to spend some time with her fiancé in a sun-drenched Arizona town. But when a wealthy local is murdered, uncovering a hotbed of deadly town secrets, Angie's getaway with her lover is starting to look more and more like her final meal.

The DaVinci Cook

Just when dilettante chef Angie Amalfi's checkered culinary career seems to be looking up, she has to drop everything and hightail it to Rome. Her realtor sister is in a stew—accused of murder. To make matters worse, a priceless religious relic is missing as well—so the Amalfi girls are joining forces in the Eternal City...and diving head-first into a simmering cauldron of big trouble.

o0o

Look for the latest Angie Amalfi mysteries and other books by Joanne Pence by visiting her website at www.joannepence.com.

WITHDRAWN

CPSIA information can be obtained at www.ICGtesting.com
Printed in the USA
LVOW10s1459110913

352007LV00015B/847/P